BROKEN
VOW

BROKEN SERIES BOOK TWO

paige press

BROKEN VOW

BROKEN SERIES BOOK TWO

STELLA GRAY

Paige Press
Leander, TX 78641

Ebook:
ISBN: 978-1-953520-56-2

Print:
ISBN: 978-1-953520-57-9

Editing: Erica Russikoff at Erica Edits
Proofing: Michele Ficht

ALSO BY STELLA GRAY

The Bellanti Brothers

Dante

Broken Bride

Broken Vow

Broken Trust

ABOUT THIS BOOK

I thought the past was behind me... but becoming Mrs.
Bellanti put a target on my back.

My husband isn't a gentle man.
And God knows he isn't the sharing type.
Rico's announcement has dropped a bomb into my
marriage.

I never thought I'd see Rico again.
Never thought Dante would ever have to know.
Seeing the way he looks at me now, as though I'm just
another problem to be handled?
It's breaking my heart.

I thought I was in love once before.

I swore I wouldn't make the same mistake twice.

But falling for a Bellanti was far worse than a simple mistake...

PROLOGUE

FRANKIE

I'VE NEVER MET a man like Rico Correa.

He's hotter than a Calvin Klein underwear model, he brings me a single red rose every time we meet, and when he whispers in my ear in *Italiano* it makes me shiver down to my toes.

And the best part is, he's all mine.

The Tuscan sun glows overhead as we walk along a path beside the sea. The water is pure turquoise here, dotted with tiny waves that sparkle like diamonds glittering on the surface. We've spent the day strolling across the sandy beach of Spiaggia delle Marze and through the cool, dappled shade of the sweet scented pines of Pineta del Tombolo.

We stop every so often to frolic in the water or get snacks from seaside vendors: bomboloni—airy Italian donuts filled with pastry cream—and cool coconut gelato, paper cones filled with a mix of fried seafood called *fritto misto*, and skewers of tomato, basil, and mozzarella drizzled with olive oil and fresh herbs. The scent of the Tyrrhenian Sea is clear and invigorating. An ancient stone wall acts as a crumbling barrier between us and a steep incline leading to the white sand below.

I pause and pull Rico close to me, then angle my cell phone high to take a selfie of us. I love the way his golden Mediterranean skin contrasts with my peachy complexion, his dark hair against my blonde, his deep brown eyes next to my blue ones.

"How did it come out?" Rico asks afterward.

"What do you think?" Grinning, I tilt the screen toward him so he can see the photo.

It turned out Insta perfect—so much so that I don't even need to use a filter. Which, naturally. We look perfect together and we're on the coast of freaking Italy.

He wraps a strong, muscular arm around me and pulls me against his chest. His heart beats steadily beneath my cheek and butterflies explode in my middle as I breathe in the scent of his cologne. It's been weeks of this, him and me, spending every free minute together. He dotes on me, gazing into my eyes as he strokes my hair or my cheek, kissing me constantly, holding my hand, calling me *bella*—beautiful. No man has ever paid this much attention to me, or made me feel like this when his mouth is on mine, when our bodies are interlocked.

That's how I know that what we have is real.

This is what love feels like.

I post the photo to my social media and then pull Rico close for another. I can't help ogling that one, too.

His jawline is amazing. So is the way his mussed hair falls across his brow.

"We are perfect together, Francesca," he murmurs in his sexy, Italian-accented English.

"I was just thinking that," I say with a smile, but when I try to show him the picture he barely glances at it.

Instead, he drops to one knee, looks up at me...and pulls out a small diamond ring.

DANTE

EVERYONE CONTINUES DANCING all around us, but it feels like this dark-haired pretty boy with the thick Italian accent has just cut my feet right out from under me.

I've stopped moving. Stopped breathing. I'm holding on to Frankie's hand, just staring at her. My wife is still as a statue, her face an open book of guilt and terror. It tells me everything I need to know. This isn't a prank.

There's a low ringing in my ears, a buzz of rage building in my body as I replay the last five seconds in my mind over and over again.

"I'm her husband."

Her fucking husband?

The interloper next to me stands there with an ease that suggests he rather enjoyed dropping that bomb. He's twirling the wedding ring on his finger, not a lick of discomfort on his face as his gaze bounces between me and Frankie...in fact, if anything, he looks smug. The prickles running down the back of my neck start to hurt.

Fists clenched at my sides, my body taut as a wire, I take a deep breath. That face of his is about to look a lot less self-satisfied.

But before I can even take a step toward him, my wife's older sister Charlie appears with a big, perfectly practiced saccharine smile on her face. Armani is at her side.

"There you two are! Come with me, come with me." She takes Frankie's hand and hustles us off the dance floor, toward the catering tent and away from the festive crowd. Armani follows behind us, smoothly but forcefully steering the pretty boy along with him.

The tent is empty, having been cleared of the buffet hours ago. There are plenty of tables and chairs, but no one seems keen to sit.

Silence falls over the five of us. Frankie tries to stay close to her sister, but I take her arm and keep her in place next to me. All eyes turn in my direction, as if I'm expected to take charge.

Fine. I'll be the ringmaster of this fucking circus. But I've got one question first.

Turning to Frankie, I spear her with a look.

"Is it true?" I ask quietly.

Her eyes glisten with tears, but she manages to hold my gaze as she nods. "I'm sorry."

Without thinking, I lash out and grab her chin, anger rolling over me. She winces, as if she expects me to act on the monstrous rage inside me.

"*Dante*," Charlie says softly. Her tone is a warning.

Tempering myself, I soften my grip. I won't take my

anger out on Frankie. I just have to touch her, to feel the fragility of her in my grip. I need to touch what's *mine*. A flash of this loser kissing her, ripping her clothes off, fucking her senseless, and putting a ring on her delicate finger plays like a horror movie inside my brain.

"What was your plan, Francesca?" I grind out. "Figured you'd con me, try to bleed me dry until you were found out?" The angry words fly from my mouth so fast I can't stop them. "Who put you up to this?"

"No one. It was a mistake." She takes a shuddering breath. "Just let me explain."

I wonder what she's more remorseful about: marrying me, or having her dirty little secret exposed? A hundred other questions burst into my head. Why did she go along with this arranged marriage of ours if she already had a husband? She could have easily backed out of the deal her father made—a deal she made no secret about being opposed to—yet she never mentioned the fact that she was unable to legally marry me. Why did she go through with it, then? Why the charade? What was her endgame in hiding her prior marriage?

What the hell was she after?

"You haven't even *begun* to understand what a mistake you've made," I say.

Armani steps closer, as if he's afraid I'm going to hurt Frankie. Fuck him. He should know me better than that. I call him off with a cutting side-eye and release Frankie. My brother moves back beside our unwanted guest with his hands clasped in front of him.

"Hey," Charlie says softly. "Let's just all take a breath and talk this...whatever *this* is...out. Okay?"

I glare. "There will be talking, but it will be in private, between this woman and myself."

It's impossible to wrap my head around how this happened. Armani ran background checks on her and the entire Abbott family before the wedding. There shouldn't have been a single stone unturned—yet somehow, we missed a giant fucking boulder.

Frankie is married to another man. She can't legally be married to me.

I look over at her alleged husband. He's calm, collected, as if he's making a social call instead of wreaking havoc. This man has touched her, taken her to bed, made her laugh...I can't stand it.

"Francesca." I use her full name again, watch her cringe. The tension between us is just about to implode when Marco bounces into the tent, a glass of wine in one hand and a huge smile on his face.

He wanders over, oblivious to what's going on. Hardly surprising. When does he focus on anything other than partying, pussy, and alcohol?

"Finally found you all—didn't realize we were playing hide-and-seek," he jokes. The boyish smile immediately drops from his face as he takes in the scene.

"What do you need, Marco?" I blast the words.

He isn't bothered by my anger. He's been the brunt of it for so long, it doesn't even faze him. "I, uh, just came to tell you the band is on their last song of the set. Almost time for the closing speech to our investors and the press."

"Of course," I say. *Just fucking perfect.*

"Do you need a few more minutes here? I can go make an announcement," Marco says, eyes darting back and forth between me and the others.

I know I have to keep it together—and I'm sure as hell not giving anyone the satisfaction of seeing me flustered or shaken. But the timing is shit. I can't believe I have to go out there right now and face the whole damned crowd with my "wife" by my side. The backstabbing, lying manipulator I just gave up all other women for. The thought twists my gut.

Even now she's still staring at me with that guilty expression, her eyes swimming with unshed crocodile tears. How dare she make a mockery of what *she herself* demanded from me.

"I'm good," I tell Marco. "You," I say to Frankie. "You're coming with me."

I can barely look at her. The hubris, the lies of this woman. To think she was already married when she'd looked me in the eye and recited vows she couldn't legally commit to. Even I wouldn't sink that low. God, I'd almost...

No. I didn't love her. And she'd made damned sure I never would.

Smoothing the sleeves of my suit, I turn to Francesca's husband and make slow work of pulling at my cuffs to keep myself from bashing his face in. He's not the only one who can play it cool. It would be unsavory to say the least for me to off him at my own party.

"Marco, please remove our...uninvited guest from the property," I say.

My brother flashes a gleeful smile. "No prob."

Marco didn't witness the entire exchange, but he seems to have caught on well enough. He steps forward and grabs the man by the upper arm, nudges him, and leads him away. Frankie doesn't bat an eye as her husband is carted off. Nor does she display any flicker of emotion at him being manhandled and forced out of here. I want to feel satisfaction at that, but I can't. I'm about to combust and I need this night to be over before I lose control of myself.

"And Charlie," I say, "why don't you head out and prep the press for the speech. We'll be there in a moment."

"Sure." Charlie gives her sister a long look before shuffling away to do as I ask.

Grabbing Frankie's arm tightly again, I turn to Armani. "That man claims to be Fran...this woman's husband. After the speech, I want you to find out who's lying here, and deal with it. However you need to."

He nods. His expression gives away nothing. "I'm on it."

If this story has roots, Armani will find them, follow them, and shred them into sawdust. It's what he does, and he's damn good at it.

"Let's go," I tell Frankie, pulling her along with me as I stride out of the tent.

"Dante, please—"

"Not another word," I say, cutting her off harshly. I can feel her start to tremble, but I really can't find it in my heart to care.

She's made a mockery of the Bellanti name. A headline like this won't go away—ever. It's going to overshadow everything we do at the winery going forward. Whenever someone mentions Bellanti wine, it will instantly bring up the scandal this woman brought upon us.

So for now? We're going to keep this façade going for as long as we can.

As we approach the stage, I paste a smile on my face and speak to Frankie without looking at her. "Keep your dirty, lying mouth shut while I give this speech. You're going to stand by my side like the good little imposter wife you are."

She's tried to take charge of our marriage the entire time, making demands, pushing her way into the family business. And I let her. In a way, this is my fault too.

I never should have trusted her.

2

DANIE

THE PARTY ISN'T QUITE OVER, but I've just about reached my limit when it comes to my temper. If I don't get out of here soon, I can't say what I might do. And in public, no less.

I keep Frankie close to my side while I deliver my closing speech. Despite the fact that my world is imploding, I don't allow a single whiff of drama to muddy the presentation. Because the second someone catches even a hint of trouble, all hell will break loose. Luckily, I'm used to hiding my feelings. Only fools let everyone know what they're thinking all the time.

Putting on a show for the investors and guests, I almost start to believe myself—that everything is actually fine. The words I say about the winery and our big plans for the future are true, and I feel them deeply. Why shouldn't I? My work is the only thing that I've ever truly dedicated myself to. And it's the one thing that hasn't let me down.

"And so, on behalf of the entire Bellanti family, I want to thank each and every one of you for coming tonight to celebrate with us," I say, starting to wrap things up.

There's a genuine round of applause, and it eases my mind slightly. People have enjoyed the evening immensely and seem to have faith in the forward momentum of Bellanti Vineyards. We've accomplished exactly what we set out to with this event. It was great for business, and I won't let my fake wife's deceit be the stain that shadows all our good PR.

"But as much as I've loved chatting with you all," I finish, "it's time for me to excuse myself and my wife now. We do have to be up early tomorrow for the pressing! Good night."

Stepping back from the mic, I smile and wave graciously, keeping a hand around Frankie's waist. It's all for show, of course.

We make our way down from the stage and through the crowd, the warmth of her body burning like a hot iron beneath my palm. But I don't let her go. I can't have anyone who looks at us tonight seeing anything other than the perfect couple. And my possessive streak has me realizing this might be the last time I'll ever touch her.

She played me so well. Played all of us so well. I'm still reeling at being so completely blindsided. Even now, she's lying with her face, her body, the perfect smile she wears for the crowd. All of it is a lie. Knowing it does nothing to diminish the ache in my chest, though.

Unbidden images from earlier this morning flash in

my mind, and I can't help remembering every last detail. I'd gone to her room at dawn, lifted her in my arms, and carried her back to my bed. Laying her out on the sheets, I'd stripped her naked and then took her more slowly than I ever had before. Explored every inch of her body. Touched her, tasted her. Kissed her from head to toe while her arms held me tight.

I can't erase the vision imprinted in my brain of her eyes locking onto mine as she came apart beneath me, the way she'd moaned my name, pussy gushing over my cock, the way she'd made me feel like someone actually loved me for myself, not my money, my power, my position—

No. We'd fucked. We'd fucked and that was it. Believing otherwise only serves as a testament to Frankie's skills at manipulation.

So now, as much as I'd like to drag her upstairs and bend her over the railing of my office balcony, fuck her until she's screaming loud enough for all the guests to hear and I'm too spent to feel the burn of this rage anymore, I won't do it. There's nothing inside her heart but deceit.

Funny, she always seemed so against being anything like her father, but I suppose once an Abbott, always an Abbott. She's no better than that slimy lowlife gambling addict.

Fuel on the flames is knowing that her supposed husband is probably kicking up his feet somewhere in town with that shit-eating grin on his face, waiting for whatever happens next. I'd like to have my brother arrange for the guy to quietly disappear and never return

—we certainly have the connections to make it happen. The only people who even know about Frankie and him are my brothers and myself, and Charlie. Hell, it wouldn't be hard to make the son of a bitch trip into a shallow grave in the middle of nowhere, would it? But what would that solve? It wouldn't change the fact that Frankie lied to me. That our entire relationship was a sham. Part of some master plan to...to what? I still can't even begin to guess what she was trying to get away with.

I shake the thought away. It doesn't matter. Frankie's husband might be disposable, but even if Frankie comes clean about why she kept her prior marriage from me, my former wife will never be trustworthy again.

She tries to move away from me now as we work our way through the guests and across the courtyard, but I pull her closer and murmur, "You're expending a lot of energy trying to get away from me, *wife*. Stay where I put you. I'm not done with you yet."

Her body stiffens, as if she's preparing to shake me off, but I only tighten my hold. The moment we get back to the Bellanti estate, I have a decision to make.

Are we truly over, or am I going to fight for her? I've already tossed around the idea of breaking the law on her behalf and helping hide the body. Equally, I'm tempted to wash my hands of the whole sordid mess. Give her back to her smug-faced husband and erase her from my life. It's what she deserves.

Every time people stop us to chat, I'm forced to continue with the polite smile and the bullshit.

Pretending nothing is wrong. Meanwhile, my urge to break free reaches a boiling point.

Finally, we escape. Our feet are loud on the gravel walkway leading to the house. Lights from the lampposts casts a soft glow while the evening wind blows warm and gentle. Were this a different scenario, the ambiance would be pleasant. Romantic even. Frankie's hair tossing in the breeze, the glow of the lights highlighting her natural beauty. But this isn't a lovers' stroll. It's the death march of my marriage.

I drop her arm without a glance in her direction, but fuck, I can still feel her on my skin. She hurries in front of me as if she can stop me, stop whatever I'm about to say or do.

"Dante, listen." She tries to snag my wrist, but I pull away.

"I don't want to hear anything you have to say."

Her jaw drops. "But before, you said that...that we were going to talk in private."

I scoff. "Well, I changed my fucking mind."

With that, I move around her and continue toward the house. Each crunch, crunch, crunch of my shoes on the gravel grates in my brain.

She chases after me, but I don't slow my pace. "Wait. Please. I know I should have told you. And I know you're confused and hurt and—"

I can't stop the cruel, hard laugh that comes out. Never in a thousand years will I allow this woman to think that she's hurt me.

"You can't hurt me," I tell her. "You'd have to *mean*

something to me to hurt me. You were useful, and now you're not. Simple as that."

We reach the porch and she crosses her arms over her chest, shaking her head. I can see tears welling up in her eyes. "I don't believe you."

"Believe this, then. You're not a partner. You never were. You were a means to an end, and even that has run its course. Your services as a pretend wife are no longer needed. Especially given the fact that our union is legally null and void."

Leaning around her, I push the front door open. Frankie starts to step into the house, but I grab her arm and tug her back, blocking her way with my body.

"Don't even think about setting foot inside this house," I tell her. "I want you out of my sight."

She freezes, her eyes gone wide. "What? Where am I supposed to go?"

I shrug. "Why don't you ask your husband that. As far as I'm concerned, you don't live here anymore."

Then I go inside, shut the door in her face, and turn the lock. A knock of guilt beats against the iron wall around my heart, but I ignore it.

Leaning my head against the door, some of the tension in my neck and shoulders releases at the sound of her heels tapping down the steps, then retreating on the gravel of the walkway. I let out a deep exhale, knowing there's no turning back now. No room for regrets.

Will she go to him? Will she crawl into some cheap hotel bed with him tonight? I've driven her straight into his arms, and I have to remind myself that it's exactly where she belongs.

I can almost hear the sound of my father's voice ringing in my ears.

Women will betray you, every time. It's been their nature since Eve.

He repeated those words to my brothers and me many times over the years, and I'd taken his advice to heart since I was a teenager. I've always used women for one thing, never truly letting them in or giving them a chance to take advantage of me. Just like my father had advised.

Until now.

And goddamn him, he was right.

What a fool I'd been to let myself believe otherwise.

3

FRANKIE

I DON'T KNOW what to do.

The last time I felt this devastatingly alone, Rico had ditched me at a hostel in the tiny town of Roccette and then never returned.

I stand in the dimly lit driveway, hugging myself to hold back sobs. The heavy turn of the deadbolt from inside was like a punch in the gut. Dante just threw me out.

And it's all my fault.

How can I blame him? I completely pulled the rug out from under him, blindsided him with a problem I should have taken care of a long time ago but didn't have the strength to. I'm not much like my mother, but the one trait she passed onto me is her ability to ignore problems until they go away. Even though sometimes, they never do. Putting blinders on means she doesn't see what's going on or have to face it. That's exactly what I did with the Rico situation, and now I'm paying the price.

I still can't believe Rico showed up here. That he had the nerve to—

Taking a breath, I clamp down on those thoughts. I can't expend the energy to blame him right now. If I do, it'll drain me, and I need to focus on more important things first—like where I'm going to stay tonight, and all the nights after it. Tears slide over my cheeks but I wipe them away, trying to keep it together. I don't want anybody to see me like this. Or worse, see me and start speculating about there being trouble in the Bellanti household. All I know for sure is, I can't just stand here in Dante's driveway, completely falling apart.

I start walking without a plan in mind, moving away from the house.

Music plays in the distance where guests are squeezing every last minute out of the festivities. I don't want to see anyone, so I head farther into the darkness, numb with shock.

How has my life gotten so fucked up? I never should have gone to Italy. I went there with a plan to make my family business better and ended up with a fly-by-night husband instead. Damn you, Rico.

I had thought I'd been in love, despite—or maybe because of—my complete lack of experience with men who showed me kindness and attention. Rico had promised to love me no matter what, vowed to be by my side for better or worse. He'd said all the right things, had promised me the moon...and after the wedding, when he found out I wasn't a rich winery heiress, he'd still called me *bella* even as he was planning to run away and abandon me.

I never told anyone I'd gotten married. Not even my sisters when they came to visit me in Tuscany. Rico was long gone by then, and I'd tucked my wedding ring safely away, too devastated to look at it again. It had taken my sisters spending the whole summer with me, late night talks over wine with Charlie, sunny days on the beaches with Livvie, evenings spent seeking out the best antipasti plates at local eateries or bright mornings visiting the museums in Florence (before the tourists flooded in), to finally come out of my depression. I'd finally confided in Charlie about my broken heart, but I didn't mention the wedding.

Truthfully, I thought that if Rico had gone away, then the marriage would, too. After all, he was the one who'd walked out on me—it was obvious he wasn't interested in maintaining any kind of relationship. And he'd taken care of all the arrangements; I hadn't needed to do a thing. I just assumed he'd deal with the annulment or divorce or whatever it was and that would be that.

A big part of me was also happy to keep my head in the sand after he left. It was just easier to pretend the whole thing had never happened than to wallow in self-pity, humiliation, the pain of being fooled so completely. So yes, like a child, I'd truly believed my past would just disappear. And now Rico Correa is back, just in time to spoil the new love in my life. A love that had just started to blossom, just started to feel like it had the potential to be...incredible. Blocking my one chance at real intimacy and ripping apart the career I was starting to weave.

I don't know if I'm more disgusted with him or myself.

Suddenly, I hear the ground crunching underfoot somewhere behind me, and I turn around just in time to see my father materialize from the shadows.

I do a double take, completely forgetting he'd even attended the event today. I saw him briefly when the festivities started, but that was hours ago and there'd been no sign of him since. Judging by his unsteady footfalls, he's been drinking all day.

"Dad?"

Before I can say anything else, he grabs me painfully by my hair, tugging a giant handful.

"Ow! Dad! Let go!"

My hands find his wrist as I attempt to get him off me, but he only tightens his hold and pulls me closer. The alcoholic stench of his breath hits my nose. Nausea roils inside me.

"I remember you slapping me," he says, his voice low and ugly.

"And you remember why I did it?" I challenge. He was so drunk that day, I doubt it.

Ignoring my question, he goes on, "You ever do anything like that again, I'll beat you black and blue."

I don't need to see if there's sincerity in his eyes. I know he's not bluffing. He's done it before and I have the slightest crook in my nose to prove it. He'd only lost control the one time, when I was fifteen and we'd come close to losing the house. If Charlie hadn't intervened and brought me to the ER, my face and body bloodied and bruised, I don't know what would have happened. She'd thought he was going to kill me. I was never totally sure she'd been wrong.

Dad hadn't hit any of us again since, but I know the violence is still in him. Always simmering right below the surface. He wears the threat of it like an expensive coat, showing it off, keeping it on display so we never forget what he's capable of. I'm staring the danger in the eye again right now.

Swallowing hard, I stop fighting, hoping my submission will prompt him to let me go. The roots of my hair twist against my scalp. He breathes heavily in my ear.

"Okay, okay," I finally say softly. "I understand."

If he's waiting for an apology, he won't get one. It wouldn't make a difference anyway.

"You're lucky Dante took you off my hands. You've been back what, four months, and I'm already tired of seeing your face."

With one last painful jerk of my hair, he shoves me away from him and stumbles back toward the party lights, leaving me to cradle the back of my scalp. Gulping down a sob, I realize that I'm behind the vineyard's offices. I hurry to the back door and punch in the access code, then make my way to the receptionist's desk and pick up the phone. My hand trembles as I hold the receiver to my ear...and start to second-guess what I'm doing.

Charlie is still running the party, but I know she'd

send her husband Clayton to pick me up right away and bring me over to their place to stay. Problem is, she'd corner me as soon as she got home later, demanding explanations—explanations that I know she deserves. Dante had kept the whole surprise ex-husband thing pretty discrete, even in the chaos of the confrontation. Which I do appreciate, but obviously it was only a temporary reprieve. Even though it's Charlie, and I know she won't judge me, I'm in no shape to spill all my secrets tonight.

I set the receiver back on its cradle and take a deep breath.

On autopilot, I make my way to Dante's office door, the knob cold in my grip. It's unlocked, the room still and scented with my husband's cologne as I slip inside. Moonlight spills through the windows, a hazy silver. I walk absently around the room, dragging my fingers on the smooth edge of his desk, hugging myself as I look out the window, my stomach clenched in grief and panic. I stumble to the leather couch on the far wall, grab the knit throw from the back, and curl up on the cushions.

Everything that's happened tonight rushes at me all over again, filling my brain and flooding my body. My scalp burns where my father pulled my hair. My heart stumbles like it's been punched. Any chance I ever had of really connecting with Dante is gone.

I pull the blanket tighter around me, but the smell of his cologne only gets stronger—and now I'm thinking of how we'd fucked on it not two days ago. I'd come in after working all day in the tasting room to find him sitting right here, going over the press releases for the upcoming event. He'd looked so intense, so sexy, that I couldn't stop myself from putting my hands all over him. Unbuttoning his shirt, sliding my underwear to the floor, hiking up my skirt to straddle him. To take him deep, his fingers gripping my ass hard, his cock grinding into me as we tried to muffle our heavy breathing. We'd loved—really loved—each other so good.

I'm getting goosebumps just thinking about it, even now. He'd been different that day. More focused on me. Maybe we weren't in love, but in that moment, I felt like we'd been on the way to something like it. Until tonight.

Now I'll never know.

Amidst all my pain, though, is the uneasiness of seeing the way Dante acted just after Rico showed up. It chills me how he'd put on a show so easily in front of people, pretending everything was fine between us, acting like the same attentive and demonstrative husband he'd been in the hours before he'd found out about my betrayal. He was so believable. The lying seemed so natural for him. How do I know that he hasn't been putting on an act the entire time we've been married? How can I ever trust his actions again?

Not that it even matters, I tell myself. He'll never let me behind that granite façade again. Whatever had been growing between us is dead and gone.

The night ticks on, and somehow I manage to fall asleep.

I'M awoken by voices outside in the hallway, feeling disoriented as I roll over on the couch and remember where I am. Everything that happened last night comes back to me in a sick rush.

I recognize Dante's voice, followed by the receptionist Ruby's softer tones. I have a flutter of panic. I didn't intend to fall asleep on the couch in his office, but I really had nowhere else to go. I'm just pushing myself into a sitting position when the door opens.

Dante walks in but I don't move, too tired and heart-sick to care. He stops short at the sight of me, his eyes pinned to my face, then dropping lower. I glance down and heat floods my face. My left breast must have slipped from the neckline of my dress in my sleep, and it's now almost completely exposed. I pull the blanket tighter around me and look away. I'm glad Ruby isn't here to see me in this state.

Clearing his throat, Dante moves to his desk and takes a seat, giving me the cold shoulder like he did last night. I feel an ache in the center of my chest as if my heart is actually bruised.

"I'm not going to listen to any begging or excuses," he says flatly.

I swallow with difficulty because my throat is so dry. "I don't have any begging or excuses in me." It's the truth.

He meets my gaze over the top of his laptop and stares at me so long and so intently that I have the urge to squirm, but I steel myself. I'm determined not to let my fear and uncertainty show. Not to him.

Finally, he looks away and begins tapping on his

laptop. He busies himself while I sit there frozen, unsure what to do next. Time and silence stretch between us. Inside I'm panicking. I have no idea what to do with my body, what to do with my life. How to get my clothes, my makeup, my things packed up. Where to go.

"I've given it some thought, and unfortunately we'll need to keep up appearances for the investors," Dante suddenly says, as if picking up a conversation we were already having. I just nod. "Luckily, after last night's performance, they're sold on us being a loving couple." His voice drips with distaste over the words.

"Okay. So...what do you want me to do?" I ask, trying to keep my voice steady. As if my entire life isn't imploding before my eyes.

"You'll be moving into the guesthouse. Maintaining the fiction of our happy marriage. At least for now."

I feel numb as I nod. "Okay."

"And you'll not ever put one foot in this office, ever again. Is that clear?"

My jaw drops. "What? This is my *job*. I've put hours of work into the—"

"Too bad," he cuts me off. "The terms aren't up for negotiation, Francesca."

Taking a deep breath, I try to start over, this time more calmly. "I understand what you're saying, Dante. But I've made real connections with our vendors, and—"

"*My vendors*. You're no longer a Bellanti, and you're not a part of this business. Going forward you'll complete only the tasks I assign you, and nothing more."

I open my mouth to negotiate, but he doesn't give me the chance.

"I'll have all your things removed from the main house by eight p.m. And for God's sake, go clean yourself up. You have a shift in the tasting room. Which will be your *last* shift."

I can't breathe.

He waves his hand pointedly toward the door, not even sparing me a glance.

"Now get out."

4

FRANKIE

WHAT A PATHETICALLY SMALL life I have.

Later that day, I supervise the movers bringing my boxes into the guesthouse. Honestly, there's hardly anything for them to carry in. I have them stack all the boxes in the living room for me to sort through on my own. Pretty much everything I'd hurriedly packed up after I finished with my shift in the tasting room was purchased with Dante's money. Clothes, shoes, accessories, makeup, and miscellaneous toiletries. My fluffy bathrobes. And...that's pretty much it. None of it is all that meaningful; none of it can comfort me in my solitude. I never imagined the sum of my life could fit into a handful of cardboard containers, but here we are.

I only needed a single box to hold the things I came into the marriage with. I have the movers place it in the bedroom. It makes me feel better to have my things separate from everything else that has the Bellanti stink all over it.

Once the movers are gone, I'm left alone to sort through my possessions. It doesn't even take an hour to put it all away, but I'm exhausted by the time I finish. The unfamiliarity and emptiness of the guesthouse is draining. It takes mental energy to immerse yourself in a new space, to get to know it and let yourself become a part of it. And I don't even know how long this place will be my residence, which drains me even more. What sense is there in expending energy trying to acclimate to a new place that will probably be temporary? I had just started to truly get my bearings inside the Bellanti house, and look where that got me.

I slowly walk through the guesthouse with my arms tightly crossed. Admittedly, the house is lovely with its arched doorways, stone walls, and terra-cotta slab floors. It reminds me of the buildings in Tuscany, infused with old world charm yet outfitted with modern trappings. I wander through the lofty living space, the two bedrooms —one a master with an en suite, the separate guest bath, a commercial-style kitchen. The house is decorated in cool neutrals and natural finishes; what it lacks in personality it makes up for in understated luxury. I feel like I'm walking through a Restoration Hardware catalogue or an *Architectural Digest* spread. Too bad there's nobody here to admire it with me.

Sinking onto the couch, all I can think about is the hollow pit in my chest. I feel so lost. And then I realize that it's late, and that I haven't eaten since this morning, when Greg took pity on me and threw together a quick breakfast scavenged from the tasting room's fridge full of ingredients for tapas and cheese boards. He'd asked me what was wrong, but I'd declined to explain. After all, Dante wanted our marriage to appear intact. All I could do was lie to Greg about having a migraine coming on and do my best to smile through the rest of my shift.

My stomach growls as I head back into the kitchen. I figure there should be at least a few dry goods in the cabinets, maybe some pasta or rice I can cook up—but surprisingly, I find the kitchen fully stocked.

The cupboards, refrigerator, and freezer are all full. Everything is fresh. Huh. Then, I see a handwritten note in the middle of the marble counter. It's tucked under a loaf of fresh baked rustic bread that's wrapped in parchment paper and tied with string. I don't even need to look at the note to know exactly who it's from: Alain, the Bellantis' personal chef.

I can feel the warmth of his good intentions as I read the note, a small smile playing at my lips even amid so much emotional wreckage. The older Frenchman was always kind and enthusiastic, eager to cook for me and make me feel welcome. The note says he'll be keeping the kitchen well stocked, and he added his cell phone number so I can call with any special requests. He's also happy to make me meals, as long as I don't tell Dante.

My eyes sting at Alain's kindness. I know he's worked at the main house for a long time. He's worked too hard, I imagine, and has loyalties to the Bellantis that should cancel out any kindness he feels toward me. Yet he'd stuck his neck out for me.

Still, I can't allow him to stumble into the center of

Dante's crosshairs. As much as I appreciate the offer, there's no way I can take Alain up on it without risking Dante's wrath. The grocery delivery itself is more than enough to be grateful for. I'll make do.

I take advantage of the fresh bread and make myself a slice of buttered toast, which is about all I think I can stomach right now. As I eat slowly at the counter, looking around the wood and stone of the kitchen, I'm reminded forcefully of Tuscany. It's not just the style of the guest-house, though. It's the loneliness and isolation.

Of course I'd loved my time there, the learning and experience of it all. And when school was in session, it had been delightful. But although I'd been lucky enough to be able to stay in a room at a family friend's house while I was in Italy, I never had much money to travel or even go out much, so I'd kept to myself most of the time. When my sisters visited, I played the exuberant tour guide, of course—but once they left I was back to my usual frugal, solitary state. Even more so after being dumped by Rico.

Yet here I am, back on my own. After being abandoned. Again.

I set down the half-eaten toast and let out a sigh. How long am I supposed to take part in this marriage façade? Forever? Is this guesthouse my permanent residence now, or is Dante going to arrange a quiet divorce for us as soon as possible? Where will I go? What will I do?

Midway through my mental panic, I hear a knock at the door. It's just after eight p.m., and I wonder if it's Alain coming to check on me.

Instead, when I look through the peephole, I see Charlie standing on the porch with Livvie at her side. Thank God for my sisters. Really, thank every God, like everywhere.

Flinging open the door, I fall into Charlie's one-armed embrace.

"What are you two doing here?" I murmur, blinking back tears.

"I interpreted your 'Dante kicked me out but I'll be fine' text as a veiled cry for help," Charlie says wryly. "So here we are."

She's got a six-pack of fancy-looking craft beer under the other arm, yet still manages to hug me back while walking us backwards into the living room. Livvie lifts up two pizza boxes as she follows.

"Garlic knots and cosmic caramel brownies, too!" she announces.

I nearly break into tears, but I'm too wrung out at this point to expend the energy. Livvie quickly arranges the feast on the coffee table, and we all gather around it, after I run to the kitchen first to get plates and a sparkling water for Liv.

As we sit together in the (admittedly very comfortable) living room and dive into the food, Charlie cuts right to the chase.

"You know I love you," she says, "but what the fuck, Frankie? What is Rico doing here? I'm on your side, but I can't really blame Dante for throwing a shit fit. What's going on?"

With a sigh, I let my head fall back against the couch

cushion. "I honestly don't know. I had no idea Rico was coming. It's such a mess."

Livvie looks between us while taking a huge bite of pepperoni pizza. Charlie hands me a beer, which I immediately twist the top off of. I take a long swig, savoring the citrus and hops. There's a beat of silence, and apparently, I don't speak fast enough for my sister's liking.

"Well?" Charlie prods. "So? Tell me everything."

I sigh. "Where do you want me to start?"

My older sister's face scrunches and I can see she's annoyed. "Your shitty Italian ex who I only know from your Instagram feed shows up in Napa out of nowhere last night, butts in between you and your husband, and apparently causes such a stink that you end up getting banished to the guesthouse until further notice. I saw the ring on Rico's finger, Frankie, and the whole situation seems really...well, fucked. Are you seriously asking me where you should start, or should I just assume the worst?"

"Can I have a beer?" Livvie asks innocently.

Charlie waves noncommittally at her. I don't know if that means yes or no, but Livvie takes it as a yes and twists the top off a bottle. The sound gets Charlie's attention. She whips a look at our younger sister. "Only half. I mean it."

"Yes, ma'am," Livvie says with a smile.

I grab a slice of pizza and take a huge bite, stalling just a bit longer before I have to pull all the skeletons from my closet. With an impatient huff, Charlie turns to her own food. We eat in silence for a few minutes, but there's definitely an elephant in the room. I hurry through a few more bites and then set my slice back on the plate.

"Okay. Here's the story." I clear my throat and lay it out, keeping my voice as matter-of-fact as possible since I know the shit is about to hit the fan.

I confess everything, all of it, from the first time we met in the market to the lightning-fast courtship to the quickie wedding...

"He was hot. He was Italian. He was sexy as sin. He claimed his father was a descendent of Spanish royalty. His mother was a famous actress, supposedly. He spoke like six languages and he seduced me with every single one of them. Brought me flowers every day. Roses. Sunflowers. Lilies."

Livvie tosses back a swig of beer and then smiles at me with a dreamy look on her face. "How romantic."

Charlie grabs the beer out of Livvie's hand and sets it on the table.

I look at my younger sister, shaking my head. "He was full of shit. It wasn't romantic at all. It was impulsive, and foolish. I thought he was someone he wasn't, because I let him sweep me off my feet without asking any hard questions. I never really *knew* Rico. Not the real Rico. And by the time I figured it all out, it was too late. I was so naïve."

"Honey, that's what love does to everyone," Charlie says gently.

"I never loved him. I was just inexperienced and infatuated. I didn't know the difference yet." The vehemence in my words surprises me. I wasn't actually sure if that was true until right now. "I have never regretted anything more in my entire life."

I wrap up my tale of woe, finishing off by describing the final moments in the hostel, when Rico kissed me goodbye and said he'd be right back with espresso and bomboloni from the corner café—and then never returned.

"So what are you gonna do now?" Livvie asks, looking a lot less enchanted now that she's heard the end of my story.

Shaking my head, I say, "Whatever I can. Whatever my real husband tells me to."

Charlie grabs Livvie's beer and finishes it. "You can start by divorcing Rico, obviously..."

"Obviously," I agree. "I should've done it in Italy, but...he was gone, where would I even serve the papers? I was far from home—even my Italian home when he actually left me. Not a citizen, abandoned by a man who said he loved me...I just couldn't even fathom trying to explain it all to a lawyer, a judge...to both of you."

Charlie slips her arm around my shoulders and holds me tight against her. "Livvie and I were in Tuscany for a whole summer. You never said anything. We would have helped."

It's all I can do to hold back tears.

"Your visit saved my life back then," I tell them. "And you're definitely doing the same thing tonight."

Hours later, after watching a rom-com and polishing

off the brownies, Livvie has fallen asleep curled up in an oversized chair and Charlie and I are cleaning up.

As I rinse dishes in the kitchen sink, I tell Charlie in a low voice, "There's something else I need to tell you. It's about Dad."

"What about Dad?" she asks, her expression turned sour. "I know it can't be good."

I proceed to tell her what happened last night, how he'd cornered me in the dark and threatened me. Charlie seems shocked, which is surprising considering the fact that nothing about our father really shocks us anymore.

"He's unstable, and he's getting worse," I conclude. "We can't let Livvie stay there with him anymore."

"Agreed. I'll move her to Nob Hill with me, indefinitely. Except the horses—"

"Maybe Delores's grandson could come and take care of them until we can find a place to move them," I say, thinking out loud. "And we'll have to come up with something to explain it to Livvie. I don't want her to know what Dad did to me."

Charlie nods. Honestly, I'm tired of lying to our baby sister. Charlie and I both know that Livvie understands more about our father than she lets on. She may be young, but she's not stupid.

"You know, one of these days we're going to have to tell her the whole story," I say.

"Yeah. Let's just let her be a kid for a little while longer, though. Life will get painful for her soon enough as it is."

I can't help but agree.

5

FRANKIE

THE KEYS to the little red Jaguar are still in my purse. I hold their weight in my palm and consider for the hundredth time what I'm about to do.

Without the car, this wouldn't be possible. I'm going to take the keys as a sign that I should proceed.

Rico has been blowing up my cell nonstop for the past few days. I haven't picked up a single call, but I listened to the first few voicemails before I started deleting them automatically—so I know exactly where he's staying.

I dress casually in jeans and a loose blouse, put my hair in a simple ponytail, and forgo makeup. I don't want to give off the wrong impression to Rico or anyone else. The last thing I need right now is to come across like I'm up to something that I'm not.

Driving to the outskirts of Vallejo, I play my music way too loud in an attempt to keep from overthinking what I'm about to do. Forty minutes later, I double-check the address on my GPS as I pull into a small, shitty motel with water-stained aluminum siding, trash littering the parking area, and a few broken-down, rusted-out cars parked beside the building. Why am I surprised? Leave it to Rico to be as cheap and inconvenient as possible.

A sarcastic scoff dies in my throat. He once promised me a honeymoon fit for a queen. Instead, he ditched me in Roccette, the Fort Lauderdale of Italy, with no money, a bunch of pretty lies, and half a bottle of the cheapest wine available in the entire country.

Looks like nothing has changed.

After carefully locking my car, I swallow my nerves, square my shoulders, and head to the door that matches the number Rico mentioned—43. I'm getting more nauseous with every step, as the mistake I made hangs heavier over my head, but I just want this problem gone. I know it's my fault—my responsibility. At the same time, it's Rico's fault too, and since he had the wonderful idea to just pop back into my life out of nowhere, he's going to help me fix it.

Time to resolve this disaster once and for all. If he's still here, that is.

I smooth the front of my shirt, toss back my pony-tail, and knock on the door. It comes out as an aggressive *bang, bang, bang*. Well, whatever. Let the whole building come running, I don't care. A few seconds later, there's the sound of a chain sliding on the other side of the door, followed by the turn of the handle. I swallow hard as the door cracks open and Rico's dark eyes look out at me from inside the room. His expression immediately lights up and he swings the door wide.

"Frankie," he says, in that overly confident way of his. "I knew you would come."

He's wearing nothing but a pair of low-slung board shorts. Of course His sculpted torso and deep olive skin are on full display, a landscape of smooth muscle that I used to constantly thrill in running my hands over. At the moment, though, looking at him bare chested fills me with distaste. I'm about to tell him to put a shirt on when he waves me inside.

I don't move. I'm taking him in, taking a moment to just look at the man who once caused me so much pain. Recalling the things I found attractive about him so long ago.

To be fair, Rico is objectively a very handsome man. Dark, mysterious, suave. He's just as underwear-model-perfect now as he was then, if your opinion hasn't been clouded by what a piece of shit he is. I can't help but notice the little trail of hair making a path down his abdomen and disappearing into the waistband of his shorts—I used to love to trace the trail and wrap my hand around the sizeable cock he's got at the end.

It's funny. I remember enjoying his body, enjoying his company, enjoying the way he took control of our relationship so that I didn't have to worry about a thing. But I remember these things the way I remember learning calculus in high school. The information is buried in my brain, but it's not worth anything to me now. It certainly doesn't affect me emotionally or physically, and it's not anything I'm going to use again. I'm a completely different person now.

Older. Wiser. Stronger.

"Come in, come in," Rico says, moving all the way back and gesturing inside. I enter but take control of the door, closing it halfway so there's still a gap open to the outside.

"What is this, *bella*? You don't trust me?" He puts a hand over his heart and gives a false grimace. "You wound me."

"I'm just here to talk." I cross my arms over my chest and stay close to the door. My traitorous eyes make one more sweep of his body and he catches me this time. A sly smile turns up his lips.

"I always liked it when you looked at me like that. I liked it even more when you touched." He spreads his arms like an invitation.

I should've known he was going to waste my time.

"I'm not here for that," I say drily, my arms still firmly folded over my chest. "We have a lot to talk about. Preferably with you dressed."

He sighs dramatically as he turns away. Heading to the suitcase sitting open against the wall, he digs through a pile of clothes and pulls on a gray T-shirt. I survey the room while his back is to me. It looks like he's ordered out from every fast-food place in the vicinity and is going for a world record on stacking the wadded, greasy bags in the tiny trash can next to the dresser. My lip curls in disgust. How could I have ever been so stupid?

Without turning around, he runs his fingers through

his hair as if he's trying to fix it. It's thick and wavy and has a tendency to get out of control. He used to slick hair oil through the heavy strands and spend an hour combing it just right. It's overgrown now, something he never would've tolerated in the past.

"Look, Frankie. The truth is—I am still in love with you." He turns around, and the sincerity in his eyes floors me. "I ran away because I knew I wasn't good enough for you. When I saw how poor of a honeymoon I was giving you, I realized I could not provide for you the way you deserve, and I panicked."

"You ran out on me," I clarify, my tone cold.

"Yes," he says, his expression remorseful. "I should have waited until I could take care of you better before making you my wife. I realized that—I knew I fucked up. So I ran. I wanted to come back to you so many times, but I promised myself I would not until I made my fortune."

I cock my head, more skeptical than actually interested. "You've made your *fortune*?"

He comes toward me with his hands open and pleading. "I came back for my first love."

"This is ridiculous, Rico." I don't have time for this. And I'm getting seriously uncomfortable.

"We had the kind of true love that poets write about, Frankie. You can't deny it. The passion between us was so intense, so fast. Love like that does not fade away. Tell me you don't still think about it." He reaches for my hand, but I don't give it to him. "Tell me you don't think about our first time."

Oh, I do. I've thought about it plenty.

Not recently, of course, but now and then. It was rushed and a little awkward, with lots of heavy breathing on his part and lots of self-consciousness on mine. All I could think about at the time was that I hoped it felt good for him, because I was sure I was in love and I wanted him to love me back. Because yeah—the younger me naïvely equated sex with love. Rico was my first real boyfriend and I thought we were going to be together forever.

Compared to what Dante makes me feel now, I know how totally wrong I was. About everything a relationship is meant to be, or has the potential to be.

Rico's dark eyes grow heavily lidded as he sweeps me with a heated look.

"I will never forget how special our first time together was," he murmurs. "How I took you to the vacant care-taker's cottage behind the Lezettis' olive grove and laid blankets on the floor...opened all the windows so the night air could caress your bare skin, poured us good wine. You were so nervous, but so passionate while I gave you pleasure again and again...with my hands, my mouth, and then I took my time making you come again with my cock. How could you ever forget I made you feel that good?"

I almost want to laugh at his heavily edited version of that night, how starkly different it is from the actual event. Sure, we snuck into a dusty old abandoned cottage that reeked of rotting timber and mildew—hence all the windows being opened. I honestly don't remember the wine, but most Italian wine is decent, so I'll give him that.

43

As for being passionate or having even a single orgasm... nope. How generous of him to paint himself as such a skilled and gentle lover.

"That's all in the past," I remind him. "I'm not interested in rehashing any of it. What I'm interested in is—"

"Okay, okay, so we will start over," he says, holding up his palms. "Start fresh. Because Frankie—I cannot live without you any longer."

Before I can reject him more firmly, he's moving toward me, forcing me backwards until I hit the door. It swings shut, and now I'm pressed against it. I look up at him with a glare.

"Rico—"

Without warning, he cups my face in his hands and presses his mouth onto mine before I can turn my head away. I go completely still, half in shock and half straight up horrified, the feel of his lips on mine so foreign yet slightly familiar. My eyes remain open as I assess how this makes me feel. It's skin on skin. But there's nothing else, none of the old fireworks—in fact, there are no sparks at all, not even a tingle of desire. Just the uncomfortable sensation of having someone much too close to me.

It's so far removed from how Dante makes me feel that I push Rico off without another thought. I wipe my lips with the back of my hand and see the flicker of hurt in his eyes. Too bad. He elicits nothing in me but pity now.

"Frankie—"

"No."

I put my hand out to keep him back as I reach behind me and yank the door open.

"But you are my wife," he pleads.

"I stopped being your wife the moment you abandoned me in Italy."

He reaches for me again, but I already have one foot out the door.

"I never wanted to hurt you," he insists. "I just wanted to be a better husband."

"Too late." A snarky laugh bubbles from my throat. "We're over, Rico. I want a divorce."

6

DANTE

Where the hell does she think she's going?

I watch from my balcony as Frankie speeds down the driveway in that ridiculous little sports car she bought. I've been out here with my coffee and my laptop since the sun came up. It's the only place I can stand to be in the whole goddamn house lately. Everywhere else just seems empty without her. I can't even sleep soundly in my own bed anymore.

Slamming my laptop shut, I move closer to the railing and watch her turn at the end of the long drive, onto the main road. The sound of the hot rod engine fades, and so does my view of her. Fuck.

My anxiety kicks into high gear, even though I know I shouldn't care. I kicked her out because she lied to me, after all, and I don't tolerate liars. Yet every moment since Rico Correa showed up claiming to be her husband, it's all I can do to stop wanting her.

What if she's on her way to him? The simmering jealousy I've been trying to ignore boils over at the thought. Pulling out my cell phone, I pull up the GPS app that's linked to every winery-owned vehicle for insurance purposes. She may not be aware, but a tracker was put on her car shortly after she purchased it. It takes a second for the GPS to register. And then the little blue dot of her vehicle begins to move southeast on the screen.

My heart begins to pound. Before I fully realize what I'm doing, I race through the doors, out of my office, and down the stairs. I jump into my car and take off in Frankie's direction, tires kicking up gravel as I speed down the drive.

I fly down the freeway, weaving in and out of traffic in a crazed attempt to catch up. I don't know why I'm so worried about where she's going, but the taunting suspicion that she's going to *him* won't stop knocking in my brain. When I see a flash of cherry red up ahead, I let off on the gas and slow the car to the speed limit. The GPS confirms that it's her. I fall back even further, relying on the tracker rather than my eyes.

But I'm losing my goddamned mind as I follow her, becoming more and more anxious as we leave the city and enter the shady city limits of Vallejo. This can't be right. The town went bankrupt a while ago and the place has fallen into a state of neglect and disrepair. Nobody comes here anymore unless they're up to no good. Maybe she's lost, or stopping for gas.

I take a right and follow a lonely street with cracked asphalt all the way to the end, where a run-down motel stretches out before me. Sure enough, Frankie's Jag is parked in the lot. I clench my eyes against a flash of anger. Jesus Christ, I was right. She's in here somewhere with him. Probably letting that oily bastard touch her.

The thought of that asshole's hands on my wife makes me—no. Not my wife. Not anymore. Fuck.

I run the fingers of both hands through my hair and squeeze my head between my palms. Then I take a deep breath, trying to convince myself she means nothing to me now. She's just a lying female who wasted my time.

Being angry at her is supposed to calm me down, but all it does is leave a bitter taste in my mouth. Gripping the wheel, I take a few more breaths to steady myself.

The sickening fact is, what's going on in that motel room is none of my business.

My anger and jealousy aren't even real, they're simply male instincts getting in the way. Testosterone and all that shit. I need to take my dick out of the equation, that's all.

I stare at the Jaguar until the car blurs in my vision. Then I get a firm grip on my emotions, methodically tucking each one into the compartmentalized recesses of my brain where all the uncomfortable feelings go. My father taught me the trick, and it's served me well. Turn it off. Put it away. Forget about it. Done and done.

Putting my car in reverse, I speed out of the lot and head back to Bellanti Vineyards. I have work to do, business to focus on. Any lingering attachment I feel toward Frankie is merely the byproduct of a poor business decision, and the sooner I wash my hands of her the better.

I park outside the offices, ignore the receptionist's

attempt to flag me down, and head straight to Armani's office. I see him standing outside his office door in the hallway, a smile on his face as he chats with Candi Gallagher. He's looking at her with the same intensity he reserves for acquisitions he absolutely has to have. But there's something more there.

Something that's going to get him into trouble if he doesn't start thinking with his head instead of his cock.

At the sight of me, Candi gives Armani a polite nod and excuses herself. Once my brother and I are in his office with the door firmly shut, he turns irritated eyes on me.

"What's this all about?" he asks. "I had another few minutes scheduled with Candi."

"You can thank me later for saving your ass," I shoot back. "I saw how you were looking at her and you need to nip that in the bud."

Armani shakes his head and goes for the coffee pot. He raises it in question, but I wave off his offer of a cup.

"We were just talking business," he says. "Can I help that she was wearing an attractive dress? What man is going to ignore that?"

I smirk. "Why do I have the feeling you'd kill any other male who happened to notice?"

He crosses the room with his coffee and sits down behind his desk. "Did you need something, Dante? Or did you just come here to stir up some shit?"

"Both, actually. Let me lay it out for you."

"I'm all ears," he says, sliding a notepad in front of him and picking up a pen.

I take a seat across from him and jab my finger onto his desk for emphasis. "The Abbott Winery has to stay with us. I've been after those vines for years. There's no way I'm giving them up. If my marriage truly isn't legit, we need to find a way to keep the Abbott grapes."

My brother takes a sip of his coffee, much too slowly for my impatient mood. I'm waiting for some response but he just stares at me. Perhaps I haven't made my case clear enough.

"Look, those vines have suffered a decade or more of mismanagement. The neglect has taken its toll, but even still, in the short time we've been tending them we've already gotten a useful yield. Those vines are resilient. Next year will be even better."

"I don't disagree," Armani concedes.

"So we'll keep the vines. Look into it. Make it legal."

He nods. "Leave it to me."

My eyes narrow. "And what the hell's going on with the Italian marriage certificate? Why's it taking so long?"

Sighing, my brother says, "Look, it takes six to twelve weeks just to get a copy of an *American* marriage certificate—and we're talking Italian bureaucracy here. Time is irrelevant to them, and there's no central government office that keeps records. I've been chasing down every local authority I can find and putting in requests for the docs, but so far it's been nothing but phone tag and extended hold times and transfers to different departments and emails that go nowhere. Point is, I'm working on it. So trust that when I *do* get a hold of someone who knows what they're doing—"

"Do they know who you are? The Bellanti name—"

"Means nothing to a sleepy records clerk in a tiny village in Castiglione della Pescaia. Swear to Christ, Dante, I'm doing absolutely everything I can. Barring a flight to Italy to go pick up the document myself, which I'll certainly take under consideration. I could use a vacation."

"Ha ha," I say dryly.

"And now, I have a question for you." He eyes me steadily and I feel like I'm about to get my ass chewed. "Will Frankie be staying in the guesthouse indefinitely?"

I cut my brother a harsh look, hoping it will shut him up, but he just raises his brows.

"I'm not trying to get involved," he says mildly. "But I need to know if I should be paying the domestic staff extra to take care of her needs as well, or if I should hire new people. The guesthouse isn't exactly close to the main house, and it isn't fair to the staff to expect—"

I get to my feet because I can't sit any longer. "Do whatever it fucking takes to keep her out of my life. She's not allowed back in the main house, period."

"Understood," Armani says, scribbling something down, his tone carefully neutral.

My emotions are showing through, dammit, but if I can't trust Armani, who can I trust?

"And listen to me when I say, steer clear of Candi Gallagher," I warn. "Don't ever fall in love. Women will betray you every single time."

He crosses his hands on the desk. His mouth twitches as if he's holding back a smile.

"So you do love her," he asks, not really asking.

"Of course I don't," I say, poker face in place again.

With that, I storm out, slamming the door behind me.

I head to my own office and lock myself inside, throwing myself into emails and calls, but my attempts to get lost in work quietly fail. My mind keeps straying to Frankie in that motel room. I curse myself for impulsively following her there.

Irritated, I stare at the wall across from my desk. The couch still has an indent in the cushion, the blanket balled up in a wad from when she spent the night in here. My brain conjures up unbidden memories of her lying there, the soft flush on her face as she sleepily watched me enter the room. The way her neckline dipped low, revealing the soft curve of her luscious breast.

I'd fucked her on that couch. My cock stirs at the memory; I adjust myself to keep my pants from pinching. She climbed onto my lap while I sat there, hiking up her skirt, spreading her thighs wide so she could sink down and take me whole in one thrust.

And there was the time I bent her over my desk—

No. I need to clear my mind of her. Put an end to this. And I know exactly what I need to do.

I need to fuck her right out of my system, and then fuck someone else. To prove she means nothing to me. That she's not special. Because she isn't.

I'll fuck her one last time.

That's all I need to make this hell stop.

7

FRANKIE

RICO WATCHES me from the doorway as I get in my Jag and speed out of the lot. I swear I can feel his eyes on me until I get on the highway, and only then do I slow down so I can think.

I'm relieved that Rico's touch brought out no reaction in me. In fact, it makes me happy to know that the hold he had on me is gone. Of my two husbands, Dante is clearly the better choice. Not just because he's rich and successful—but because even if he doesn't like me, or understand me, he's never abandoned me.

Well, at least not until he thought I betrayed him. Which, I didn't. Well, but I kinda did. Fuck, I can't keep anything straight in my head right now. Not telling him about Rico was a form of betrayal. There, I'm owning it.

I never imagined the day I said "I do" to Dante that I would come to respect him the way that I do. I don't agree with everything he does, and frankly his attitude drives me insane. The constant tug-of-war between us has become so routine that I suppose I'm used to it, but I have to admit...I also enjoy the challenge of it.

Regardless of recent developments, the fact is that when Dante and I are together, we bring out the best in each other. Professionally and personally. At least, that's the image I have of our relationship in my mind. When I think of it that way, I believe it. I truly do.

I snap out of my whirlwind of thoughts just as I'm passing the Alvarezes' fruit stand. On autopilot, I turn onto the gravel driveway and park my car outside the building. Delores is wiping down tables with a cloth, and she glances up as I pull in. A smile brightens her friendly face and she holds her arms out to me for a hug as I get out of the car.

Without me even saying anything, Delores pulls back and nods to herself knowingly.

"Whatever the problem is," she says, "you, my dear, need to feel useful again."

With that, she disappears inside the stand and then comes back a moment later to throw an apron over my head and shove a basket of freshly harvested corn into my arms.

"Come," she commands, leading me into the building's back kitchen.

We wash up first at the large stainless steel sink and then settle ourselves on two chairs that face each other, a wastebasket between us on the floor. Then, together, we strip handfuls of pale cornsilk from the ears and into the trash, careful to leave the green husks intact.

"Busy hands quiet the mind," Delores tells me sagely.

I grin. "Or maybe this is just your way of conning me into some free labor."

Silence falls between us as we work, but I know not speaking is her way of easing me into conversation. She never presses. She is a master at waiting, at patience, at always being ready to listen. There's never been a time in my life that I haven't spoken to Delores about my problems. Even so, I wonder what she'll think of me when I spill my guts about Rico.

"I got married when I was in Italy," I say as I work. "I guess it was a secret up till now."

Out of the corner of my eye I watch her, assessing for any reaction. But in true Delores fashion she just continues with the task at hand, her expression open and nonjudgmental.

"It all happened so fast; I never thought it through," I go on. "I thought I was in love. And I thought he loved me. But he ditched me on our honeymoon, and I never saw him again. Except then out of nowhere he showed up at Bellanti Vineyards the other night, to crash our press event. Dante kicked me out."

That elicits a frown. "Where are you staying?"

"Oh, I'm fine. I moved into the guesthouse. Maybe permanently, I don't know."

I huff out a short laugh and rip into another cob. Delores just nods, her concerns about me allayed for the moment.

Haltingly, and then all in a rush, I talk about my love and fear of Dante, my constant worries about Livvie, and basically what a complete dumpster fire my life is right now. I leave nothing out. My knuckles began to ache from the constant grip and pull of the silk, and I almost sigh in relief to find the basket is empty. I go to the sink and rinse my hands off beneath cool, soothing water, still talking.

When I'm finally done, I look over at Delores expectantly. She's taken out a large wooden bowl and is mixing spices together in it to make her signature blend. I get the butter and two knives, setting them on the table in preparation to dress the corn. Dropping into my chair again, I stab a knife into the block of butter.

"So?" I prod. "What do I do?"

The older woman puts the bowl on the table and sits back down, nodding slowly. Finally, she says, "One question: Do you love Dante or Rico?"

"Dante," I answer at once. "But I shouldn't. I know that. I mean—I married him for practical reasons. To save my family's winery and protect Livvie. Charlie and I are pretty sure he intended to marry her off instead if I didn't go through with the wedding. I couldn't let—"

"You married this Rico for love. And you married Dante for practicality. But it seems that things have turned on their heads," Delores states, cutting to the heart of the matter per usual. "You love Dante. Fight for him."

Right. As if it's that easy.

I fall silent again as we begin dressing each ear of corn with pats of butter and her spice mixture. Then we tie them up with hemp twine. I brood, not sure what to say or what to think.

Finally, I set my knife down. "Okay, how? How do I fight for him?"

"Girl, you got the nicest set of titties I've ever seen. Use 'em!"

My eyes go wide, a laugh bubbling out of me in disbelief. "Delores Alvarez! You're terrible."

We have a good laugh, but once we've calmed down, she gets serious again.

"Frankie, I saw how he looked at you at the pressing event. The whole night, you could just see how much he adores you. He barely took his eyes off you."

That has me smiling, but then I remember that he only felt that way for half the night. Before Rico's arrival changed everything. It seems our performance for the rest of the evening was enough to fool everyone—even Delores. My confidence starts to erode again.

I LEAVE the fruit stand with a bundle of elote to take home, a thank you from Delores for my help. As I drive the short distance back to the Bellanti estate, I form a plan. I'll go straight to the guesthouse and put on the purple dress that I swore never to wear again—the one that Dante loves so much. I know how good it looked on me and I need every advantage here. I'll wear my hair down the way he likes. Then I'll go over to the main house and explain everything, tell him I'm divorcing Rico immediately.

I make a list in my head of all the ways that Dante

and I are better together than apart. Of the value we add to each other's lives. I can't be punished for a simple mistake on my part, can I? Plus, I'm a middle child, a natural diplomat—and I'm supremely comfortable in a peacekeeping role. I've had years of experience talking my way out of things. I'll make him understand that I made a poor decision, yes, but that it doesn't have to affect us going forward.

I shower, shave, use body scrub until my skin feels like silk, lotion every inch I can reach, and basically use every trick I know to make my body soft, smooth, and touchable. Then I dress and do my hair, blow-drying it into soft waves that tumble over my shoulders.

Making my way confidently toward the main house, I see Dante standing out on his bedroom balcony, surveying his dominion like the friggin' Lion King.

There's no way he can miss me walking down the gravel drive from his vantage point, but his granite face is inscrutable at this distance.

When I get to the front door, I'm surprised to find it already open for me. I step inside and slip out of my heels. Then, taking a deep breath, I tread quietly upstairs.

This is going to work. I just know it. I'm ready to unleash all of my feminine energy and love onto him. He'll recognize my sincerity and be open to talking things through.

I feel a flicker of happiness, of hope, as I enter his bedroom and stride across the carpet. Through the French doors leading to the balcony, one of them half open, I have a perfect view of him. I slowly walk closer, mentally willing him to turn around and look at me. But he doesn't.

My self-confidence begins to waver.

I pull the door open wider and then cross the threshold onto the balcony. He's so close...right there by the railing. My nerves well up and try to get the best of me, but I swallow them down.

I'm doing this for us. I hold my shoulders high and smooth back my hair with one hand. He finally turns to face me, our eyes locking. I'm wearing my biggest, warmest smile. But it quickly fades as my hope drops to my feet.

Dante's face is completely devoid of feeling.

8

FRANKIE

THE LIGHT BREEZE blows my hair in tendrils around my face. My dress billows around my legs. Neither one of us moves otherwise.

My insides twist in knots and I suddenly realize why I'm so nervous. Dante's looking at me like I'm prey.

He's going to devour me, and not in the way I'd planned.

"I—I came to say..." I stutter.

He moves lightning fast, pushing me up against the glass of the balcony door. Before I can cry out, his lips crash onto mine, hard and hot and bruising. As he kisses me, I feel like I'm falling backwards—because I am. Dante has opened the door behind me, and his strong grip on me is the only thing keeping me upright as he devours my mouth.

My knees are so weak that God help me, I stumble, but of course he catches me. For a moment I'm exactly where I want to be. Safe and protected, back in Dante's arms. But then he picks me up roughly and carries me into the room to throw me down on the bed.

I don't have time to breathe as he tugs at my dress, quick and not exactly kind in his movements. Then the fabric rips, the sound of fine silk tearing loud in the room. It only seems to spur him on. He doesn't just tear the dress to get it off me. No, he pulls the seams apart on each side, then rips the flutter sleeves and halves the plunging neckline. He's purposely destroying it, throwing shreds of material to the floor as if he's tearing apart an enemy.

His intensity scares me. I'm tempted to push back, but his animalistic intensity keeps me in place. I'll let him use me however he wants and then we can start over. He'll see just how good we are together...

"Dante?"

Without responding, he tugs me into a sitting position and yanks my bra so hard, the band cuts into my back. I nearly yelp but keep quiet as he rips apart the fasteners and peels it off me. When I lean back and reach down to remove my underwear, he shoves my hands away, yanking my panties off. I look up at him, naked and vulnerable, my pulse pounding so hard I'm gasping.

"Is this what you came here for?" He sits back and stares at my body while working his tie loose, hurriedly unbuttoning his shirt. "You think I'm going to get my cock into you and forget about what you did?"

Yes. No. I don't know anymore.

I've never seen him like this. I'm afraid to push him, so I don't respond. Instead, I lower my eyelids in a sultry glare, doing my best to look like the sex goddess I was trying to be.

My nipples peak painfully as he strips out of his suit, revealing the strength of his chest and the tight bands of muscle over his abdomen. I grow needy and wet as an ache tugs at my center, consuming me. He looks hungry enough to devour me whole.

And I want him to.

His cock is fully erect and thick, a glisten of precum wetting the tip. Spreading my legs, I wait for his next move. He starts to climb over me, but pulls back harshly, his eyes narrowing.

"Where did he touch you?" he asks, his eyes raking my body.

The demand and rage in his words make me shiver, but I'm confused. "What?"

His hands come down on either side of my head, his palms pressing into the pillow. "Where did he *touch you?*"

It clicks then, what he's asking. I shake my head. "Nowhere. We didn't—I mean he kissed me, but—"

The look in his eyes has the rest of my words dying in my throat. God, if I could take back what I just said, I would.

I don't get the chance to try to smooth things over as he kisses me again, punishing and almost cruel with his mouth. I welcome it. Anything to erase the memory of Rico.

Dante kisses me until my head fills with the lovely,

desperate, drunk sensation. But all too soon, he pulls away from me and wipes his mouth with the back of his hand. As if he's scrubbing my taste away. I reach for him, but he moves between my legs and thrusts his fingers into me savagely. I arch my back and cry out as he goes straight for my G-spot, his fingers rapidly bringing me to a breathless frenzy.

He doesn't kiss me again, but the quick assault of pleasure on my nerves pulls me under and I swim in the feeling. The stirrings of a hard orgasm begin to build. I open my eyes and see that Dante has his cock in his hand. He quickly strokes as he works me, head glistening in his tight grip. It makes my mouth water. I want to touch him. To taste him on my tongue.

"I want to suck you," I whisper thickly, heedless of the desperation in my voice.

He doesn't respond, just looks away from me to reach for the drawer in the nightstand. He takes out a condom and makes quick work of putting it on. What the...? He's never worn a condom before.

Some of the pleasure fades from my mind. Does he think I lied about being with Rico? Or has he changed his mind about having kids?

He pushes into me while I'm still running through questions, though it only takes a second for me to get back in the moment thanks to the exquisite, thick feeling of his cock stuffing me full. I wrap my legs around him and try to lose myself in the sensations, but something is off. He doesn't kiss me while he fucks me, doesn't touch my breasts or tease my clit. Our only real connection is his cock pounding inside me, and as good as it feels, there's a lot missing.

My thoughts keep my orgasm far away, and for the first time, I don't finish before he does. Dante hardens and comes with a groan, pushing himself up on his hands instead of pressing into my chest like he normally does.

Immediately, he pulls out of me and takes off the condom, tossing it in the trash before cleaning himself with his discarded shirt. My skin cools, my pulse picking up and not in a good way. This isn't what I'd expected. Dante is so...different.

Turning back to me, he stares at me almost desperately, breathing hard. I push up on my arms and grab the sheet with one hand, but he rips it from my grasp.

"You don't get out of this that easily." He pushes me down and moves between my legs again, pushing my thighs wide apart and diving his tongue to my center. Lapping at me, sucking, stroking into me with his tongue. It's so intense, all I can do is moan and writhe on the bed.

"You're going to come, do you understand?" he says.

I can't answer him. My throat is dry, my brain under water as I ride the waves and crests of sex. Tongue thrusting in and out of my hole, he uses his thumb to stroke hard over my clit, followed by a lighter, softer touch, repeating the pattern over and over until the orgasm drags out of me, hot and strong. The sheet bunches in my hands as I ride the wave, whimpering.

"I'm coming," I tell him, trying to give him the show of obedience he demands.

But he's not done with me. He continues working my

sensitive flesh, fingers sliding into me, even as I shudder with aftershocks. I almost can't stand it, but I resist the urge to pull away as another orgasm builds, agonizingly deep.

"Again. You're going to come again," he says.

I murmur my agreement.

"You're going to say my name," he tells me.

I'm concentrating so hard, needing to come so bad, I almost don't process what he said.

"Dante," I whisper desperately.

"Again. Louder."

"Dante, yes, fuck, Dante," I moan.

He replaces his fingers with his tongue and licks me hard, relentlessly, until I can't help grinding against his face, my orgasm close, tantalizingly close, if I could just get a little more—

"Dante!" I cry out as my release crashes into me.

The sound of foil ripping open, the weight of him between my legs. Suddenly, he's fucking me again, riding me hard, pinning me down in my lingering state of pleasure as he pulls another orgasm out of me. It's hard and quick, just a firework of release that has another one immediately behind it.

His hand wraps around my throat. "Say my name, Francesca."

I'm more than happy to comply—he's pushed all possible thoughts of anyone else into oblivion. "Fuck! Dante...oh my God."

"Come for me," he repeats, over and over, in perfect time with his cockthrusts.

Just like that I'm coming again, senseless as it crashes over me. He groans and pounds three quick thrusts into me, his release pulsing inside my swollen channel.

Then he collapses, lying on his side, his head beside mine and his breath warm and harsh in my ear. It's so peaceful being here with him, I can almost believe we've turned a corner.

Not to mention, that was insane. I can't even count how many times I came. He's a beast. And I love it.

A smile tugs the corner of my mouth up as I lean in to kiss him. But his eyes immediately open and he recoils, quickly getting up off the bed.

"I want you gone," he says.

My stomach drops, my face going hot. He's throwing me out? After what just happened?

The rosy afterglow quickly fades as the reality of my situation sneaks back in.

I sit up and try my best to look unbothered. "Okay... I'll go back to the guesthouse."

He gives me a smile of pure distaste and shakes his head. "No. You're not a Bellanti anymore. You never were, and you're certainly not a guest here."

My jaw drops. I feel like I'm sinking. Drowning. "But —I thought we had to keep up appearances for the—"

"Fuck appearances, and fuck the investors. I don't care anymore. Go back to your loser father for all I care." He jabs a finger in the air. "But he still owes me. I'm keeping the vineyard."

Dante goes into his bathroom, his voice reaching out at me.

"I'm changing the name, though. The Abbotts mean less than nothing to me and I'll be damned if I keep that name."

I clutch at the sheet in fear, pulling it up to my neck. All I can think about is Livvie and the horses.

Swallowing hard, I find the willpower to make my voice strong. "What about the house?" Despite my attempt at bravery, my tone wavers.

"Oh, you didn't know?" Dante scoffs, his head popping out so he can sneer at me. "Daddy Abbott kept that for himself. Though I'm sure it's only a matter of time before he loses that, too."

My mind is racing, but I'm immobilized by panic.

Dante comes out of the bathroom, still stark naked, and spreads his hands at me. "What are you still doing here?"

I look at him, but I don't see him past the veil of tears in my eyes. Sliding out of bed, I spot my ruined dress in a heap on the floor. I'm not sure how much of it is even intact, so I just wrap the sheet around myself with as much dignity as I can muster.

Tears rolling down my cheeks, I quietly let myself out.

9

FRANKIE

My FATHER WILL KILL me if he finds out that I invalidated the terms of his debt settlement with the Bellantis. Or maybe he'll just turn Livvie directly over to Dante, or go on yet another bender so he can gamble away every remaining cent we have left. Knowing my father—and unfortunately, I really do—he'd probably do all three.

Which is why I'm going to spend the night at Charlie's place. I'll try to figure out what to do from there. Returning to my dad's house would be the stupidest thing I could do. I'll have to act like everything is fine for as long as possible. Dad'll get tipped off at some point, but hopefully by then I'll have a plan in place.

In the guesthouse, my suitcase lays open on the bed, waiting to be filled. I feel paralyzed as I stare at the closet full of clothes that I don't even want. I can't believe I thought my life couldn't get any smaller...because here it is, shrinking yet again.

Ignoring all the clothes paid for with Dante's money,

I dig out a box in the corner of the closet that holds what remains of my original wardrobe. It isn't much, but it's mine, and after I change into an old pair of jeans and a college T-shirt, I dump the rest of the contents into my suitcase. After a moment's hesitation, I decide to take the marabou-trimmed lavender robe too.

I toss in my toiletries, then zip up the half-full bag and head into the living room. Grabbing my purse off the couch, I dig out the keys to the Jaguar. I really love that car, but it is essentially Bellanti property and if I'm not going to keep the damn clothes, I have no business keeping the car. It would be crass, wouldn't it? I jingle the keys in my palm, feeling their bittersweet weight in my hand before I set them on the coffee table and turn away.

At the threshold of the front door, I stop and look down at my rings. I twist them off, my heart breaking, and then tuck them into a zippered compartment of my purse. I'm not done with Dante yet. Until he demands them back, I'm keeping them.

The phone is all mine, though (thank you, phone insurance), and I use it to dial an Uber to Charlie's. She said she'd be happy to have me, but I still feel guilty for imposing on her like this. My sister has her own life to live, after all, and I never intended to rely on her as much as I have been. Still, I'm beyond grateful that I have her.

The Uber estimate for the trip is over two hundred dollars, and I curse under my breath. I'm not sure how much money I have to my name at this point. It's likely that the bank accounts are locked, the credit cards frozen, and I only have access to the very small amount in the personal account I came into the marriage with. It certainly isn't enough to rent a place, or even pay for a hotel for a few days. If it wasn't for Charlie, I don't know what I'd do. But I don't have a choice. I need to get out of here.

The Uber app lets me know my driver is thirty minutes away—fuck. I don't want to stay in this guest-house for one more second. I'll just start walking to the vineyard's front gate. Anything to get away from the man who just broke my heart. I run a hand through my hair and secure my bag over my shoulder, then hoist my suit-case and step out into the sunlight.

As I make my way over the gravel drive, I start to wish I'd taken a hot shower first. I can still feel Dante on my skin, still smell his cologne on me. Dammit. That'll be the first thing I do when I get to Charlie's. Take a scalding hot shower, then maybe have a shot of whiskey and a cup of herbal tea. Then bed. I can't wait for this day to be over.

Halfway to the gate, I hear a car coming up behind me, engine purring, gravel crunching under its tires. Please, God, don't let it be Dante. I keep my head high, my eyes forward, refusing to turn around—but when the car pulls up along my left side, passenger side window rolled down, I see it's not Dante at all. It's Armani.

"Where are you headed, Frankie?" he asks gently.

"I have an Uber coming."

It's a noncommittal answer. I'm not sure how much Armani knows, but I'm exhausted and humiliated and upset—I don't want to say more. I keep walking.

"Wait," Armani says. I stop. "Can I give you a ride? It's the least I can do, after my brother's been such a prick. Please. I want to help."

The kindness in his tone touches a nerve. I feel my resolve sinking. Especially considering the fact that I can't really afford the Uber anyway.

"Okay," I concede with a nod. "Thank you. I was on my way to Charlie's."

"You're welcome. Your sister lives in San Francisco, correct? Nob Hill?"

I nod again. "If it's too far, I can—"

"Not too far at all," he says, putting the car in park.

He gets out and takes my bags, putting them in the back seat. Then he holds the passenger door open for me before getting back behind the wheel.

"I just need the address for my GPS," he says.

I recite it for him as I put my seat belt on, then cancel my Uber.

The car is brand new, the leather seats comfortable and warm. I feel myself begin to relax for the first time in hours. The trip from Napa to San Francisco will probably take about ninety minutes, but I get a soothing vibe from Armani which I know will help my nerves on the drive. He's as calming as Dante is terrifying.

Once we're on the freeway, we pass a billboard for a local family restaurant called The Monkey House, featuring a monkey holding a pizza in one hand and a pair of roller skates in the other as he hangs from a tree by his tail. It's a pretty popular spot for kids' birthdays, similar to Chuck E. Cheese but with a much larger alcohol selection for all the frazzled parents.

Armani points to it offhandedly. "Used to be our favorite place to go when we were younger."

I hitch a brow. I can't imagine Dante roller-skating to save my life. "Really?"

He smiles. "The Bellantis have lived in Napa for generations, but my brothers and I were sent to private schools on the East Coast. We didn't spend a lot of time here during the school year, so we don't have a ton of childhood memories of the area. But whenever we came home for summer break my dad would have one of the staff bring us to The Monkey House to blow off some steam. We always had the best time."

It's kind of comforting, to think of the Bellanti brothers as normal children, doing all the things that other kids do.

He looks at me again. "What about you and your sisters? Did you ever go there?"

I shake my head no. "We spent more time going to harvest festivals, county fairs, horse shows—that kind of thing. My oldest sister was a cheerleader all four years of high school, so I'd go to all the football games. Livvie does dressage so we traveled to her events a lot, too."

"Horses were a big part of your life growing up."

"Yeah." I pick at the hem of my shirt. "One of our favorite things to do was ride our ponies through the vineyard..." My voice trails off as a burst of sadness punches right through me. I can't think about Livvie and the Abbott Winery right now.

Armani drops it, seeming to understand. We drive a few miles more before he gives me a sideways glance. "Can I ask you something?"

"Sure."

He pauses as if trying to choose his words carefully. "Why didn't you say anything about this Correa guy before? I didn't get the impression you were chomping at the bit to marry my brother. You could've easily gotten out of it."

"I was embarrassed," I admit. "I made a really dumb mistake when I was living in Italy which basically resulted in me getting abandoned in the middle of nowhere on my so-called honeymoon. I never saw him again."

"I'm sorry," Armani offers.

"Me too. I tried to just bury the whole thing and move on with my life, which I thought was a great idea at the time, but as you can see, it completely failed."

I go quiet as I start to tear up a little, and Armani reaches over to awkwardly pat my hand. I'm not used to genuine kindness from men, and his attempt to comfort me is strangely touching. I blink hard, looking out the window. Does Armani understand what it's like to be at the whims of a dangerously selfish man? Does he know how it feels to sacrifice yourself for a sibling? Glancing over at his profile, I wonder.

With a demanding, autocratic brother like Dante, perhaps Armani and I have more in common than I thought. I'm sure their father Enzo was just as terrifying as Dante, if not worse—which makes me feel like I understand Armani in some small way. Like I can trust him.

"The whole thing was such a whirlwind, I don't know how we even had time to make it legal," I continue haltingly. I tell him about getting swept up in young love —my first real relationship and about our impromptu wedding ceremony in Tuscany. "As for marrying Dante... I guess I thought I was doing the right thing to protect my family's interests. Though it hasn't exactly turned out that way."

He smiles and offers some sympathetic words of understanding, which I'm grateful for. I wish Dante would listen the way Armani does.

Before long, we arrive in San Francisco and drive up the hill toward my sister's home. Armani gets out to grab my luggage, then waits in his car at the curb to make sure I get in safely. As Charlie opens the door and ushers me inside, I turn to see Armani giving me a little wave before driving away.

Livvie is asleep already, but Charlie makes us tea and we sit on the couch while I fill her in on all the details of my failure at being a sex goddess to win back my husband.

"It's all over," I tell her. "My marriage, my job at the vineyard, the Jaguar, the Abbott property—all of it's gone."

She runs her finger around the rim of her mug. "I suppose my job as the Bellantis' event planner is gone, too?"

"I'm sorry," I say. I know how hard this is hitting her, too.

Her house on Nob Hill was a gift from one of her husband Clayton's family connections. Clayton makes some money working for the mob, sure, but it's always in fits and spurts. Charlie's job with the Bellantis was supposed to be the steady one...not anymore, though.

"What about the End of Harvest Gala?" Charlie asks. "We've already sold a ton of tickets. Do you think Dante will cancel it?"

The Gala is another venture that Charlie had dreamed up and proposed to Dante when she brought up the idea for the original First Press event. Since the pressing event had been such a huge success, we'd assumed End of Harvest would be, as well.

Charlie seems to take my silence as a confirmation of her fears.

"Oh God," she says, hands in her hair. "I'm gonna need to call all the vendors tomorrow, get everything canceled. I hope I can get the deposits back. And we need to refund everyone's tickets, too, and see if we can offer them something as an apology, maybe a coupon or—"

"Shh, shh, hold on, hold on," I say. "Don't do anything yet. I'm going to talk to Dante tomorrow. I'll smooth everything over. I promise."

I hope I didn't just lie to my sister. But all of this is my fault, and I have to make it right.

I married Dante to save my family, but it looks like I

may have set the stage for destroying them. I take my sister's hand in my own.

"Everything's going to be okay," I assure her.

How many times can I keep saying that before I stop believing it's true?

10

FRANKIE

My LITTLE SISTER glances over at me for the millionth time but doesn't say anything. I know something's up. She's been fiddling with the strap on her backpack for the last half hour.

I borrowed Charlie's car this morning to take Livvie back home so she can visit the Abbott stables and take care of the horses. After that, she'll catch the bus for school. Livvie promised she'd stay under the radar, but I'm still worried about her. Dad isn't usually up this early, though, and she won't need to go into the house—so she should be fine. At least, that's what I keep telling myself as we make the drive from Nob Hill down to Napa.

When I turn onto our old street, I tell her, "I'll be back to pick you up tonight around dinnertime. Make sure all your work is done by seven, okay?"

She doesn't agree.

"Livvie?" I prod.

"Actually, um, I was thinking," she says haltingly.

"Maybe I should just...stay over at the house tonight? I mean, I can sleep in the old stable master's quarters. Dad never goes in there. He won't even know."

"Hell no," I reply.

She sighs. "But it's ridiculous for you and Charlie to be driving all the way here every morning and night. That's like, three plus hours round trip. It must be costing a fortune in gas."

"No." I'm resolute. "I'm sorry, and I know it sucks, but please trust me on this."

"What if something happens to one of the horses?"

"The Alvarezes stop by to check on them every night," I remind her gently. "I don't blame you for being worried, but the horses are in good hands. I promise. This is what's best."

My sister is quiet for a moment. "Why are we doing this? Is Dad getting...dangerous again?"

And there it is. The insight into our messed-up lives that I wish my baby sister didn't have. Charlie and I have tried so hard to protect Livvie, but it's foolish to think we can keep anything from her. Even though nobody her age should have to worry about their parent becoming violent or getting involved in shady deals, trying to hide things from her doesn't make them go away. Besides, she's too smart for that. Nothing gets past her.

I grip the wheel tighter and clench my jaw. I might not be able to lie to Livvie, but I don't want to upset her further, so I just nod and don't elaborate.

Her warm hand covers mine. "I'll be ready by seven on the dot. I'm sorry."

"Nothing that has happened is your fault. We just want to make sure you're safe. And the horses too."

We're at the mailbox now, so I turn off the headlights and drive slowly down the packed dirt of the driveway in the cool blue pre-dawn. The grass is overgrown, there's some trash scattered in the ditch along the driveway. My heart sinks to see these two subtle signs that things are falling apart again.

Livvie unbuckles her seat belt as we pull up to the stables. Giving me a long look, she hoists her backpack on her shoulder and then gets out. I watch her go, waiting for the light to turn on inside before I roll back up the drive.

My middle is clenching with anxiety. I hate leaving her here, but I want her to have some normalcy too. But something else has been bothering me, so I don't immediately turn back onto the street again. Instead, I park near the road and turn the car off. My anxiety goes into overdrive at the thought of what I'm about to attempt.

I shouldn't have the urge to vomit over entering my childhood home, but I do.

Making my way toward the house, I walk as quietly as possible over the dewy grass. The sky is beginning to lighten as the sun comes up, so I know I have to be quick and silent. I'd rather not get caught sneaking around the house in broad daylight.

Carefully, I use my old key to unlock the door to the mudroom, wiping my sandals off carefully on the mat. Then I stand there for a good ten seconds, listening hard for any sounds or signs of my father. The air is free of the scent of coffee. All the lights are out. It's now or never.

I pad down the hall toward my dad's office, caution in every step, knowing full well that this is a really, really bad idea. But it's probably my only chance to get what I need and get out. Thank the gods, my dad left his office unlocked. I creep inside and close the door behind me, raking my eyes over the filing cabinet. My heart is pounding so hard, I can feel it in my chest. But I only need one thing, and I'm pretty sure I know where to find it. Assuming my father hasn't made a mess of things since the last time I was here.

Holding my breath, I yank open the third drawer from the top. There, filed away in the far back, are the documents relating to my marriage. I pull the entire file out and flip through the paperwork until I find a copy of the marriage contract that Dante and I had to sign. I slip it out and quietly replace the file, then fold the contract into thirds before tucking it into my waistband.

Sweat beads my hairline as I tiptoe out of the office. I've just closed the door behind me when I hear a creaking in the hall. I freeze, flattening myself against the wall, but I see nothing in the shadows. Swallowing hard, I hurry back the way I came, out the side entrance, and run for the car. I don't think I breathe again until the mailbox is disappearing in my rearview mirror.

On autopilot now, I drive directly to the Alvarezes' fruit stand. It's a little busy this time of morning. There's a line of people waiting to get coffee and breakfast sandwiches for their morning commute, so I let myself in through the back door and fill up a cup of strong black coffee before going back out and sitting at a café table in the early sun. Delores sees me and gives a little wave before returning to her customers. Moments later, she rushes over with a guava pastry, giving my shoulder a squeeze before rushing back to the register. Just that small gesture is enough to imbue me with a sense of calm. I'm safe here.

Taking a few deep breaths, I turn to the contract, sipping coffee and devouring the flaky pastry as I carefully read over the convoluted legalese filling the pages. And then, I see it.

"... transferal to Francesca Carina Abriana Abbott and Dante Bellanti *or* her legal spouse..."

I have to read the sentence again.

I can't believe what I'm seeing here in black and white. The contract doesn't simply stipulate that the winery belongs to Dante free and clear—its ownership transferal is dependent on me *being married*. My father's signature effectively transferred the Abbott Winery to me and my husband in a 50/50 split. Something Dante never deigned to tell me.

My hand is shaking as I set down my coffee. What a fool I am. How could I have not read this contract in depth until now? These pieces of paper bind my life.

But wait.

I read the line again, the words sinking in with a clarity they hadn't before.

Or her legal spouse. Not Dante.

Which means one half of the Abbott Winery actually belongs to...to *Rico*.

I try to grab my coffee but fail. It topples over, spilling

hot liquid over the edge of the table and onto my leg. I barely notice, still in shock as the truth of what I've just read crashes through my mind again and again. I own half the winery, and Rico owns the other half.

Dante doesn't own a goddamn thing.

Leverage. That's what this is. Dante will have to talk to me now. I'm determined to make my case.

I feel numb as I get up from the table and head back to the car. I can't think straight as I drive to Bellanti Vineyards. I need to figure out exactly what I'm going to say to him, but the words won't come. How could he keep this information from me? This entire time, he acted as if he owned me...when in reality, his ownership of the Abbott grapes was *dependent on me.*

Before I can overthink it, I park the car in the gravel drive and head to the Bellanti offices. He's going to listen to me. He has to. If he wants this winery, he'll have to deal with me.

I'm trembling with anxiety and excitement and a weird type of hope as I tap in the keycode on the door. The little light flashes red at me. Maybe I typed it in wrong. I try the code again, more carefully this time, and get the same result. What the hell?

I'm about to text Armani to let me in when the door suddenly opens from inside. I'm relieved, until I glance up from my phone to see Jessica's smirking face.

"You've been relieved of your duties here at Bellanti Vineyards," she says. "I'll try to remember to send your final paycheck to...do you even have a home address, or...?"

I don't have time for this shit. I try to push past her, but she moves to block me.

"Get out of my way," I snarl. "I need to talk to him."

She looks me up and down and then smirks. "He's not interested."

The innuendo in her voice pisses me off even more.

"I think he'll be *very* interested in what I have to say, actually. And didn't he fire you?"

She laughs, but I just take advantage of the moment to push past her and storm inside the building. I make sure to raise my voice loud enough that I know Dante or one of his brothers will hear it. I don't care if I make a scene.

"I'm here for the financial records for Abbott Winery. Which, according to my marriage contract, I co-own with my husband."

Jessica appears in front of me again, her arms crossed. "Dante is not your husband."

I smile. "Oh, I know. Which means, legally, he has zero claim on my family's winery anymore. Or maybe I should call my lawyer for clarification."

I yell that last part real loud. There's a shuffle of footsteps and Dante suddenly appears in the hallway, flanked by Armani and Marco. I wave the marriage contract in the air.

"Read your contract, Dante. You don't own one goddamned Abbott grape."

No reaction from him whatsoever. That granite face again. I wish I could smash a wine bottle into it. A thick one.

Everyone is silent as Dante storms over to me, closer and closer until he's towering over me. I hold my ground, glaring up at him with my shoulders thrown back and my chin high. His jaw grinds side to side before he speaks so low that only I can hear him.

"You still owe me, Francesca. Your family still owes me."

"We'll pay," I tell him. "On our terms."

He smiles at that.

"You sure will."

11

ΓRANKIE

ON MY WAY back to Vallejo, I try to figure out what to tell Rico to get out of this without losing half my life—and half the Abbott Winery—to him. I need to convince him that a quick, painless divorce is the best thing for both of us. A clean break, an amicable parting of ways. We've grown apart, we have dissimilar aspirations, we're different people now...all the usual irreconcilable differences. Thank God he doesn't know about the winery stipulation my dad put into my marriage contract. If Rico knew he was entitled to half the property, I'd never get rid of him.

I also need to figure out how to pay Dante back without...fuck, how much do we even owe him? I've never seen a number, but knowing my father's gambling habits, his debt to the Bellantis has to be seven figures or more. I mean, surely I'm worth at least that much. Even so, it makes me sick to know my father is capable of putting dollar signs over his daughters' heads.

And sicker to know I'm only worth something to the wrong man.

Pulling into the shitty motel's parking lot, I refocus on sorting through what I need to do now. Obviously I still want a divorce, but what if Rico won't agree to one? On the other hand, staying married to Rico long term isn't an option—not when he's proven himself to be such a lowlife. But in the meantime...I need to weigh all the pros and cons.

Ultimately, as much as I hate the idea of it, the least worst option might just be pretending to reconcile with Rico in order to keep the Abbott Winery in the family, rather than in Dante's hands. After all, my only hope of generating enough cash to clear my family's debt to the Bellantis *is* the winery. Is it possible to get the place operational again, back to the level it used to be?

There was a time when my parents made decent money. The winery was prestigious, and Abbott wine sold very well. Once my father stopped being able to fill purchase orders, though, everything had a domino effect. Our reputation suffered, sales lagged, profits dried up. The winery fell into disrepair. Without money to pay workers, the grapes weren't harvested properly and the vines were allowed to overgrow. Some of the buildings are in urgent need of maintenance as well. But for the most part, I'd say most of the damages are fixable. There is nothing catastrophically wrong with the winery that would prevent us from making wine again.

My heart begins to pound when I think about it. Is it

possible that Abbott wines could make a comeback? Hell, maybe I can trick Rico into signing the winery back over to me. Or I can conveniently "find" an old document specifying that neither Rico nor I are entitled to the others' property in the event of a divorce. Assuming that Rico doesn't try to fight me in divorce court and just goes back to Italy, he'll never find out. Can you go to jail for falsifying a prenup?

I've never been one for manipulation, but it seems I've gotten pretty good at it, unintentionally. Day by day I'm turning into less of the person I used to be and more into someone like Dante. The only difference is that Dante is well versed in getting what he wants out of people through intimidation and persuasion, and he has Armani by his side to navigate—or circumnavigate—the legal system in order to back it all up. I have no one to help guide me through this. At least not in the way I'd need to if I want to get rid of Rico once and for all.

I guess it all comes down to this: I can't risk splitting the business with him in court. It would inevitably result in a public sale, since I can't afford to buy out his half of the winery—and thus I'd lose my chance to pay back Dante. So, Mrs. Rico Correa it is.

But the thought of going through the motions, even temporarily, turns my stomach. Reconciling with Rico means I'll have to live with him, eat with him, sleep next to him in the same bed. He's going to want...sex.

Oh. God.

Breathing slowly through my nose, I push away those

thoughts and square my shoulders. One moment at a time. I need to stay focused on getting the winery back to work. I have to do this for my sisters. For Livvie.

I get out of Charlie's car and walk toward Rico's motel room, fighting the urge to run every step of the way. I don't even get a chance to knock, though. The door flies open as soon as I'm outside and Rico stands there with both arms spread wide in greeting.

"Frankie!"

He pulls me in before I can recoil and kisses me on both cheeks. His hands cup my shoulders and he all but drags me across the threshold before kicking the door shut. I smell the dying fragrance of his antiperspirant as he wraps his body around me for a bear hug.

"I heard the good news!"

I have no idea what he's talking about but I can't stand here with him touching me a second longer. I shrug out of his grip and take a step back. "What good news?"

He gives me an amusedly sly smile. "Oh Francesca, don't tease me. I know you came here to tell me. We are co-owners of the Abbott Winery!"

"What—but how—who told you that?" I stutter. I'm stunned. How the fuck did he find out? *I* just found out, for Chrissakes.

"Facebook!" he says merrily.

"What?"

He takes me by the wrist and leads me to a seat at the single table in the room where his laptop sits open. I watch him click a few things on the social networking site and then turn the screen my way so I can see the message he received through Facebook Messenger from Jessica Madsen. Dante's assistant sent Rico a fucking Facebook message?

Of fucking course she did.

"How do you know her?" I ask.

"We met at the Bellanti event," Rico says with a smile. "She is the one who told me where to find you. I met many of your colleagues that night."

I bite back my rage as I read the message she sent Rico, timestamped just after I left the Bellanti offices not even an hour ago.

"SO MANY CONGRATULATIONS to you and Frankie on your co-ownership of the Abbott Winery! The whole office just heard the happy news! The Bellanti Vineyards tasting room will miss her as an employee, of course, but we know you two have a bright future ahead!"

I try to school my features so he doesn't see how this is affecting me, but I have a feeling I'm failing. Of course Rico would have made connections with everybody at Bellanti. He probably schmoozed his way around the whole event before he even bothered to ask about me. I can only imagine how many names and contacts he collected from my coworkers. Not to mention how many free glasses of wine he took advantage of.

That's how Rico works. He worms his way into every part of your life with his good looks and his sweet words and that damned Italian accent. Add in some well targeted compliments, some shared interests, a few bull-shit stories that have you thinking you know him much better than you really do, and suddenly he's your best friend, all in the blink of an eye.

Little do you suspect that the whole reason he works so hard getting to know you so fast isn't because he's genuinely interested in you. It's because he's trying to find your weaknesses so he can use them against you. To get what he wants.

"So, how much do you think we can get for it?" he says, snapping me out of my brooding.

I blink. "Excuse me?"

"The winery! How much do you think it is worth? We will list it right away since we might have to wait for a buyer, and we will sell off all the equipment sepa-rately. Or we can cut up the land into cheaper parcels, I bet those will sell faster." He's pacing as he talks, full of energy and excitement over the fortune that just landed in his lap. "Maybe we just auction it off to the highest bidder in a short sale, no? Even if we do not get what it is worth, we will still make millions. Just think, we can finally have enough money for that honeymoon, ha ha!"

The more he goes on, the more I realize that he doesn't give a shit about me, or the winery, or anybody but himself.

"Oh, I met a real estate guy at the pressing event, too —a developer!" he adds, nodding to himself. "He said he was looking for land to build a new subdivision. We can make a killing selling to a developer like that. Maybe they will even name it after us. Correa Estates. Correa Ridge. Correa—"

"Rico, stop." My face is hot, flushing with anger, and I get up from the chair and cross my arms over my chest. "What about my family? My older sister is an event planner for the winery right now, so where is she supposed to go? And my little sister keeps her horses at the Abbott stables. She rides there. We can't just sell off the whole property out from under them."

He shakes his head with a patronizing smile. "Frankie. Millions of dollars can buy lots of new horses. And your family would not have to work! In fact, you will never have to worry your pretty little head about anything ever again. I will take care of everything for you."

I know he's lying. I've heard all this—or some version of this—before. And I recognize the gleam in his eye, too. It's the exact same frenzied, half-manic gleam I saw the last day we were together back in Italy.

I'm struggling to keep my breathing even. I'm struggling even more not to let loose on him.

"Come on, Frankie." He comes over and puts a placating hand on my shoulder, giving me that boyish look. The one that used to make me do anything for him. "I am your husband. I just want what is best for you, don't you see that?"

There's no doubt in my mind: Rico Correa is getting ready to cut and run. He'll take whatever he can from me and then leave me in the dust. He doesn't give a shit how things will turn out for me. He only cares about himself.

I shake his hand off and storm out without another word. He shouts at me to come back as I make my way across the parking lot, but I don't turn around.

Once I'm back in the car, I peel out of there as fast as I can.

At least when Dante used me, he had the grace to tell me to my face.

FRANKIE

WELL, that was a shitshow.

Not that I'm surprised at how my visit went. We're talking about Rico, after all. "Shitshow" should be his middle name.

I need to talk to Dante again. Get him to tell me what kind of price tag my father put on my head. There's no way I can even begin to start planning how to pay back my family's debt when I have no clue how much my dad owes the Bellantis.

But getting Dante to see me won't be easy. Nothing is easy when it comes to him.

The fact is, every single car that passes through the gates of Bellanti Vineyards is seen by dozens of pairs of eyes—as well as cameras and security guards—before it gets anywhere near the house. Now that I've made such a loud (and very public) scene in the Bellanti offices, I'm sure everyone at the vineyard knows I'm not welcome there anymore...so I can't just roll up and hope to get past

Jessica again. Security guards would surround my car before I even set foot on the gravel driveway. Fuck.

There's only one way I can think of. I don't know how else to get in. But this plan of mine is about as insane as going to see Rico this morning...

Guess I might as well go two for two on the insanity scale and just get it over with.

I'm going to have to sneak onto the property from the Abbott compound.

My father's truck is nowhere to be seen as I roll down the driveway and pass the house. Outside the stables, I wait in the car for a few minutes to make sure the coast is clear, just as I did when I dropped off Livvie this morning. It sounds ridiculous, but I can't help worrying that my father is going to come running out from somewhere waving a gun at me. When nothing happens, I take a deep breath and head into the building.

"Ytse," I call out softly as I make my way down the center aisle.

My horse's dark, glossy head swings over his stall and he greets me with a whicker.

"There you are," I coo, stroking his nose. "That's my beautiful boy."

I quickly saddle the big black gelding and change into some of my old riding clothes that Livvie keeps stashed in the office for me. Then I write a quick note, telling my sister that I'm going for a ride and might be a little bit later than planned, but to stay in the barn until I get back.

"Do you think I'm crazy for doing this, Ytse?" I ask as I mount up.

The horse just stomps his foot, snorting as if he's impatient to get going.

Laughing, I pat his neck and nudge him out of the stables. He prances a little, letting me know he's eager to gallop. Good. So am I.

"Of course I'm crazy," I tell him. "My whole fucking life is crazy."

I keep him in check while riding him out of the yard and toward the vineyard. Once we're out in the vines, I give Ytse his head and we take off, flying over the verdant hills. It's exhilarating, and my chest aches at the realization of how much I've missed this. With the sun on my back and the wind in my hair, I almost feel like I can outrun my problems for a little while.

But all too soon, the split rail wooden fence that separates the Abbott and Bellanti vineyards comes into view.

I don't slow Ytse down. His ears perk forward as he spies the fence. He knows what to do.

He makes a lead change and then gathers himself right before soaring over the rail like the champ that he is. Just like that, I'm on Bellanti property. We only get a few strides before I see a group of men in the vineyard out of the corner of my eye. It's Marco and a few other workers, staring at me slack-jawed. Shit. I never expected to see one of the brothers out here.

Keeping my head high, I give a jaunty wave as we trot past them, praying that Marco doesn't have his cell phone on him or else I'm screwed.

I ride to the edge of the vineyard and crest the ridge that peers out over the Bellanti estate, spread out across the green valley. You can see everything from here. It's breath-taking. The low rise edging down to the stately home. The vineyard buildings. The winery itself, the tasting room. All interspersed with immaculate grounds, beautiful flowers, and well-tended trees. It looks like a postcard. It's probably a good thing this view neglects to show the poison inside.

Taking a deep breath, I tell myself I can do this. I really can. Because after my failure to get anywhere this morning, I simply can't afford to fail again.

I nudge Ytse down the hill and over to the seldom used, fully fenced-in tennis court. It's the perfect place for him to soak up the sun and wait for me. I jump down and loosen the girth of his saddle so he'll be comfortable.

"Don't be afraid to leave a big pile of shit anywhere you want, sweet boy."

Making sure to latch the gate behind me, I cross the wide lawn and make my way toward the rear of the main house. Praying that the door leading to the kitchen is unlocked, I reach for the knob and let out a breath when it turns easily in my hand. I'm in luck.

Peeking my head around, I strain my ears for any sounds from within. The scent of steel cleaner and blueberry muffins fills the space, but everything is silent. I slip in and quietly close the door behind me. Making my way across the room, I'm almost to the door leading to the main hallway when I pause to check my watch. Five-thirty. Good. I still have a half hour before—

Suddenly, the door swings open and Dante storms in. I take a step back with my eyes wide, bracing myself on the countertop. His expression is as dark as his suit, his brows tightly knitted together.

"I thought for sure Marco was high, but here you are. What the fuck are you doing in my house?"

Of course, Marco would have his phone on him. He can't risk missing a text from one of his booty calls. Or ratting me out to his brother. Dammit. There goes the element of surprise.

I stand a little taller and force myself to meet his gaze. "How much does my father owe you?"

His eyes sweep over me. "What?"

"How much. Does my father. Owe you?"

My skin is heating beneath my riding pants and long-sleeve shirt. Some of it is frustration, but the rest is all arousal. I can't be in the same vicinity as Dante and not want him. It doesn't matter that he's looking at me like I'm an insect beneath his shoe. Or that every word that comes out of his mouth will be dripping with venom. It doesn't matter that he despises me.

I still want him.

He doesn't answer at first. He almost looks wary of me, in fact. But he recovers quickly. "He owes me a winery."

"Cut the bullshit, Dante. Give me a number."

"Three to four," he says.

"Three to four...*what*? Hundred thousand? Three to four million? Three to four what?"

Dante takes a step toward me. It's deliberate. Measured. I hold my ground.

"The number of times I'm going to make you come," he finishes.

Those words derail every thought in my head. It takes me a second to regroup. "I'm...I'm not here for that. I'm here to talk about—"

"Of course you are," he says, standing directly in front of me now, close enough that I could touch him. "You could have just called. But you didn't."

His gaze is so intense that I have to look away.

"And you would have actually taken the call?" I scoff, trying to play it cool.

"Guess we'll never know."

Dante takes the last step, closing the gap between us, the familiar musk of his cologne making my pulse race. He slides his hand up my arm, down my chest, cupping my breast and running his thumb over my peaked nipple so I shudder. Before I can stop myself, I let out a soft gasp. I didn't think this through. I didn't think any of this through. He can't know how much I want him. And I can't give in, no matter how much he makes me want it.

"Come to bed with me, Francesca," he commands.

I shake my head. "I'm not your wife."

"I don't care," he says. "And I know if I slid my fingers into your hot little cunt right now, I'd find it doesn't care either. I know what you look like when you're soaking wet. It's written all over your face. Come to bed with me."

He flicks my nipple, and I hiss. "No."

"Then I'll have to fuck you right here."

All I can do is stare at him. I feel like a deer in headlights, knowing I should run, but unable to. My body can't seem to obey me. I do nothing as he presses my back against the counter and slides his hand down the elastic waist of my riding pants.

"Like I was saying," he murmurs, thrusting two fingers into me and pumping them so his thumb presses against my clit. I am, of course, extremely wet.

There's no gentleness as he finger fucks me. It's hard and fast and intentional, and fuck, my body goes haywire. I widen my stance, spreading my legs to give him better access. I've missed this so much. Sex with the devil is addictive, and the withdrawals have been torture.

Gripping his shoulders, I lean into his hand, seeking the pleasure he's offering even as I hate myself for it. He swirls his fingers, working me hard, changing the rhythm but not the pace. Then his head dips low as he rests his forehead against mine, closing his eyes, sighing deeply. It almost feels tender. Almost like he loves me.

Suddenly an orgasm rips through me so fast and hard that my knees buckle. I moan, clinging to his shoulders as his arm wraps around me, holding me in place. I blink back tears as I ride out the shockwaves. I'm gushing.

"Your married cunt just came all over my hand," Dante says. "You're a fucking cheater."

Ice water on the fire.

I twist out of his grip and stalk away, but he comes up behind me and pulls me against him so I can feel the hard ridge of his arousal pushing into my ass.

"Let me go," I grind out.

Instead, he bends me over the kitchen island, positioning my hands on the butcherblock, and says, "We're not done."

I don't protest as he wrenches my pants down to the tops of my riding boots. I hear the clink of his belt. The rough drop of fabric. The tearing open of a condom wrapper. Jesus, I want him so bad I could cry, I want to impale myself on his cock, ride that hard length. I want—

"You might be married to Rico, but your cunt belongs to me."

His filthy, hurtful words feel like a physical touch. My pussy aches with need, pulsing as if he's already stroking my clit. Dante puts a hand on my back and presses me flat against the butcherblock. The tip of his cock bobs against my slit and then rams home, his thick shaft filling me in one thrust. A tortured moan leaves my mouth at the feel of him stuffing me, and I realize I'm already coming again, clenching tight and fast around his cock.

A self-satisfied laugh ripples in my ear. "Two for two. That didn't take long."

Bastard.

He starts fucking me deeply from behind. Slowly, with measured, intentional movements, making us both shudder and groan with every thrust. My breasts rub against the countertop, my nipples tingling at the friction, my hands gripping the island for traction as my hips pound against the edge. I'll probably have bruises tomorrow, but I don't care.

"You filthy, dirty whore. Look at you, spreading your legs for me. I'm barely inside you for two seconds before you're coming all over my cock. And I'm about to make you come again. Admit it, Francesca. You want this."

"Fuck you."

He laughs again. "Fuck me? Oh, you are. And you're doing it so well."

Jesus Christ. Another orgasm flashes, quick and hot. I can't moan or move, suspended by the force of the pleasure. He rides me through it, his cock swelling, growing harder. Stretching me to the limit. It's over all too soon, but my clit pulses and pouts with the rise of yet another orgasm as Dante thrusts hard. Once. Twice.

"I love fucking my whore. Pounding that tight little pussy, making you scream."

Fuck. I come again. So hard that my body shakes, the orgasm almost painful this time.

Dante digs his fingers into my hips and slams into me so deep, I feel like he's splitting me apart. I squeeze my eyes shut as he finally lets go with a groan, his face pushed into my shoulder. I feel so shaky, I don't know how I'm still standing.

Looking up, I catch his reflection in the window as he lifts his head from me. His face is etched with emotion. He looks utterly decimated. Devastated by what he's just done. Or maybe it's just regret.

Quickly pulling out, Dante turns away to throw out the used condom and adjust his clothes. I'm still struggling to tug my pants back up when he throws a dish towel at me. It lands on the island, and I look over at him.

"If your husband wants to negotiate with me, he can do it himself," Dante says. His mask is back on, his expression cold. Completely devoid of anything but distaste. "I don't negotiate with cheating whores."

For a moment I'm speechless, before managing an affronted, "*Excuse me?*"

"Go on and bring him around. He can watch me fuck your brains out if he wants."

With that, he glides out the door, leaving me to clean myself up.

I do the best I can, shaking the entire time.

13

ΓRANKIE

I SIT TENDERLY in the saddle as I guide Ytse in a slow walk back to the Abbott compound. My mind and emotions are in a tumble after leaving Dante, but I still have enough clarity to recognize screaming when I hear it. It sounds like a woman, or a young girl.

Livvie?

Adrenaline rushing through me, I spur Ytse to a gallop. We've just crossed over the property line when the noise of a diesel truck and lots of shouting reach my ears. Something's going on at the house. As I get closer, my fears are confirmed. I clearly recognize my little sister's voice. She's crying, pleading with someone.

My heart lurches to my throat as I squeeze Ytse's sides even tighter with my calves. Comprehending right away, he picks up his pace, clearing the ground in long strides. I'm gripping the reins so tightly now, my fingers are going numb.

We crest the ridge behind the stables just in time to

see a few rough-looking men loading what's left of the Abbott Friesian stock onto a huge horse trailer. Scanning for Livvie, I see her cornered against the outside wall of the building. She's beside herself, screaming, tears streaming down her face as she's held back by a burly guy who doesn't seem to care that her entire world is coming apart. I'm going to be sick.

What the fuck is going on?

This has to be Dad's fault. It always is.

I nudge Ytse down the ridge, kicking up gravel as we make our way toward Livvie. I realize my mistake all too late as one of the men points at me.

"That's the missing one!" he calls to the others as he jogs over, his beefy hand taking hold of Ytse's bridle. "We got 'em all now."

Before I know it, I'm pulled off my horse, my struggling and protests no match for the man who has his hands on me. Rage has my pulse rushing in my ears, my skin itching all over. It takes all my willpower to stop myself from fighting back, kicking and screaming. But I don't want anything to happen to my sister, so I hold still, breathing hard, and wait it out.

There's nothing I can do but watch as they roughly remove Ytse's bridle and saddle before shoving a halter over his head and leading him into the trailer, alongside the leggy four-year-old that Livvie's been training for dressage.

"Not Max! Please, please leave me Max!" Livvie begs. Her desperate, agonized voice ripping my heart to shreds. "Please, just one!"

The men are unmoved.

I'm dying to go to my baby sister, try to comfort her in some way, but the beasts won't let go of us. There's nothing we can do but watch, helpless, as the trailer's metal doors are slammed shut and latched with a clank. One of the men heads back to the idling truck and climbs into the cab, motioning to the others.

"Time to move out!" he shouts. "Let's go!"

With that, Livvie and I are finally released. My sister sinks to the ground in a heap and buries her face in her hands, sobbing as if someone has just ripped out her soul. I run over to her and fall to my knees, wrapping my arms around her and holding her as tight as I can.

I feel strangely numb, a faint buzzing overriding all of my senses as Livvie's tears soak through my shirt.

As the truck pulls the horse trailer down the drive, leaving a cloud of dust in its wake, Livvie pulls away and wipes her eyes with her forearm. I help her stand but keep my arm around her as we watch the trailer disappear from view.

Yet another piece of our lives lost to our father's obsessions.

"I hate him," Livvie says, her voice resolute. "I hate him so much, Frankie. I swear to God, I never want to see him again."

I have no words to comfort her with. There is literally nothing I can say or do that will fix this. I can't believe Dad did this to her—she was the only one of us who hadn't turned away from him. And for what? Another gambling debt? A bad card game? Payment for sleeping with some bookie's wife?

We collect a few of Livvie's things from inside the house—photos, some clothes, the few pieces of modest jewelry that Charlie and I have gifted her over the years —and pack them into Charlie's car. Conveniently, Dad doesn't show up the entire time. He's so sadistic that I'm honestly a little surprised he wasn't here to watch his youngest daughter's agony as he took away the only thing that mattered to her.

Both of us are silent as I drive us back to Nob Hill, but I hold her hand the whole way. I texted Charlie before we left to let her know what happened, and she's waiting for us at the front door when we arrive. I notice that her eyes are rimmed in red as she pulls Livvie into a hug, nodding when I tell her I'm bringing Livvie's things up to the guest room.

Charlie and I spend a few hours helping Livvie unpack. We've agreed that it's best for her to live permanently at Charlie's place, even though the commute to school will be killer.

"I'm sorry. I just really can't go back there," Livvie says, her chin trembling.

"Don't be sorry," I tell her soothingly. "Charlie and I can take turns with the driving."

Charlie nods. "It's no big deal."

Livvie swipes at her eyes. "He's a monster. I don't want to spend one more night under the same roof as him. Not that he was home most nights anyway."

I look over at Charlie, who shoots me a worried look.

Dad's obviously still drinking and gambling, which means he's also racking up new debts left and right. We need to find a way to stop him. He's already lost everything, but Livvie herself is still a commodity, and there's no way in hell we're letting him sell her off, too.

We make mac and cheese—Livvie's favorite, though she barely touches hers—and binge episodes of *Gossip Girl* in the living room until Livvie tells us she wants to go to bed. I watch her climb the stairs, sadness wafting off her like perfume, and can't help noticing how much older my baby sister seems all of a sudden.

Charlie taps me on the shoulder and tilts her head toward the kitchen.

"Come on. Dessert."

Shaking my head, I say, "I'm not—"

"We're drinking it," she clarifies. "I have an excellent red."

"Oh. Well, in that case."

We end up sitting on the kitchen floor with our legs crossed, leaning against the lower cabinets and passing a bottle of wine back and forth. She's right. It is an excellent red.

"So," Charlie says. "What happens next?"

I take a long swig of the wine and pass it back. "Maybe I do sell the winery. Cash out our entire family history and, you know, write off six generations for a payout. A chance at a future...but then Rico will get half of it. Fucking Rico."

"Fucking Rico," Charlie agrees. "I wish we knew what to do with that guy."

I smile bitterly. "Oh, I have a few ideas. Not that any of them are legal."

"Clayton's line of work isn't exactly legal," Charlie reminds me. "Just say the word. I guarantee you he knows a guy."

"I wish it were that simple." I huff out a laugh, then go quiet. "I hate to say it, but Dante would know what to do."

Sighing, I lean my head back against the cabinet. I can feel my sister's eyes on me.

"He's really gotten to you, hasn't he?" She passes me the bottle, and I take another drink.

"I never knew I could hate someone and love someone so much at the same time," I tell her. "But I feel like I ruined it before it even began, thanks to all this Rico bullshit."

"Maybe," Charlie says, holding her hand out for the wine. "Dante's kind of an asshole, though. No offense."

I have to laugh. "You're not wrong. The thing is...I know it sounds hard to believe, but before Rico came out of the woodwork, it felt like Dante and I—we were becoming something real."

"Oh?" My sister cocks a brow, watching me take a greedy drink from the bottle.

"Don't get me wrong, Dante *is* an asshole," I admit. "A huge asshole. But...I don't know. At first, all we did was butt heads. But at some point, I realized that we both seemed to enjoy the...challenge of each other. And then the work I did for the winery—it earned me his respect, too. Because even though I had to fight him every step of the way, I was good at the job."

"You were great at the job," Charlie points out.

"Yeah," I say with a nod. "I proved myself. Maybe I shouldn't have had to, but I did. And it made Dante trust me. As for the physical stuff, we're compatible in that way also."

Charlie giggles. I don't elaborate. My cheeks are hot enough, and not just from the wine.

"*Anyway*," I go on. "The point is, when I married him, I went into it thinking I was just doing what I had to do. Going through the motions. And now...everything's different. I had no idea what he would become to me. What we would become."

Charlie nods. "At least you knew who he was when you married him. There wasn't any love clouding your vision. I married Clayton because of love. I mean, I don't regret it, but..." She looks down at the bottle in her hands, giving it a swirl. "It's really hard not knowing where he is when he disappears for days and weeks on end. And it's even harder not knowing if he's going to come back. Trusting that he isn't doing something terrible. Knowing he probably is."

"I get it. I do." I've had the same thoughts about Dante.

"He says he's never killed anyone, but..." She trails off, her eyes clouding with some distant memory. But then she snaps to and takes another drink. "I love him anyway. He could probably kill a hundred people and I think I'd still love him. Can you believe it? What the hell does that say about me?"

"I'm sure Dante's ordered his fair share of hits," I tell her. "It comes with the territory. Doesn't change how I feel about him, though."

"Dad really screwed us up, didn't he?"

"That he did."

Charlie laughs, and I join in. I feel like we've never been more connected.

She salutes me with the wine. "To shady men, and the women who love them."

Then she takes a swig and passes it to me.

I hold the bottle up in a toast. "I'll drink to that."

14

DANTE

DINNER IS A TASTELESS NECESSITY.

All I can taste is Frankie. The residue of her skin is full on my lips and tongue, and my mind is on a loop replaying the scene in the kitchen in excruciating detail, down to the way she felt in my arms, around my cock, the scent of her hair, her lustful moans.

Until today, I'd been haunted by the last time we slept together. How she'd been wrapped up in my bed sheet like a Greek goddess, cheeks flushed with sex, her eyes glowing. Thanks to her unexpected visit today, now all I can envision is her long legs in those tall riding boots, her curvy ass hugged by tight jodhpurs. Her eyes flashing bright with anger. She's always the best fuck when she's angry...God, I hadn't been able to help myself. And when I'd slid my fingers into her hot—

"Dante?"

I look up to see Marco and Armani staring at me. That's when I realize I'm holding my fork in a death grip, even though the table has been cleared and dinner is over.

Apparently, judging by the looks on my brothers' faces, it's time for serious discussion. Alain makes a quick round at the table, pouring us all cups of coffee and setting out dishes of sugar and heavy cream. I take a deep drink of mine, black and steaming, wishing it would scald Frankie right out of my memory.

But of course, it's the perfect temperature. Our chef knows his trade well.

I'm on edge, with a restlessness I haven't been able to shake for days. My interaction with Frankie has only made it worse. Might as well bring up the constant elephant in the room. The one none of us have been eager to face.

"What do we know about the man who killed our father?" I ask, pushing thoughts of my former wife to the corner of my mind and mentally begging her to stay there. "This...George Bregman."

Just saying the name out loud puts me in a foul mood. Armani clears his throat and coolly reaches inside his breast pocket. He pulls out a piece of paper and slides it across the table to me.

"These are known associates for Bregman," he tells me. "A couple of them are interesting."

I unfold the paper and scan the list of handwritten names, some vaguely familiar. Except—one of these names has my pulse picking up. I find myself rubbing my finger over it. A Bruno. This name came up a lot when my mother and sister went missing years ago, in the boating accident. Not to mention, it's the surname of a notorious rival crime family.

"Let me see that," Marco says. "Please."

I pass him the page and look back at Armani. "Have you contacted any of these?"

"Not yet," he says. "I want to gather something concrete first. Bregman owes most of them money, but that's as far as I've gotten."

Just having the name of the man who killed our father is enough for me. I'm ready to make a move.

He's likely got protection, though. We'll have to lay a trap, draw him to us. The kind of game our father was well versed in playing. Growing up, I remember men being led to our front room by his enforcers. The captives would be crying. Pleading. Apologizing. And all the while my father would just stare at them, expressionless. Once he had what he wanted, they'd be taken away. It took a long time before I realized that he probably hadn't simply let them go.

Marco sits up straighter. "What about the Bruno family?" he asks, homing in on the same name I did. "You have to look at who stood to gain the most with Dad out of the picture."

Armani hesitates but then shakes his head.

"It's possible, but not likely. Dad and the Brunos went way back," he muses. "I won't say they didn't have their tensions, but they're an old family like us. They know how it works. It'd be too big of a risk to fuck with the Bellantis that way. Retaliation from us could wipe them out completely, not to mention screw their relations with all the other families who respect us."

"Let's keep an open mind regardless," I suggest. "Even if they didn't hire Bregman directly, we can't assume they weren't involved in some way. They're a huge syndicate."

"Understood," Armani says. "I'll keep up the investigations."

Marco volunteers, "I'm gonna be looking into a few leads myself. I've got some things I want to check out."

My coffee cup hits the table with a clatter. "Like what? You know something you're not telling us, Marco?"

"Nothing like that," he says. "Just due diligence."

I give a nod of agreement and drum my fingers on the table.

"What have you come up with to deal with the Rico issue?" I ask Armani.

His lips pull into a thin line. "I'm still working on it, as you're well aware. Unless you'd rather handle him the old school way? The way Dad would've handled it?"

It's obvious what he's asking me, and Marco looks between us almost eagerly as I think it over for a moment. Dad would have had Rico erased in a heartbeat. But I'm not trying to be my father. Enzo Bellanti I am not. Part of me is surprised Armani even made the suggestion.

Granted, we have an unspoken agreement whereby he has free rein to take care of select problems however he sees fit—but my brothers and I have been on the same page about keeping our family name clean ever since our father passed. And as much as I want this Correa asshole out of our lives, I don't want to cast any new shadows over our business or our family name. Especially now that the winery is flourishing.

"No," I tell him. "We're staying clean. Just keep doing what you're doing."

I see Armani's shoulders relax as he lets out a breath. "All right. Agreed."

Marco looks slightly disappointed but nods his agreement as well. Armani stands from his chair and excuses himself for the night. Marco finishes his coffee a few minutes later and heads to his room as well.

I'm left alone, brooding, my coffee now cold. Everything in my life is always so goddamned cold. Except for Frankie. She was warm and lively. She challenged me with her intelligence and her mulish stubbornness. A stubbornness I'd grown to grudgingly respect. And I wasn't the only one, either.

Hell, she'd only worked in the tasting room for a short while, but I can tell that the staff miss her. Those genuine smiles I'd started seeing around on the Bellanti employees are long gone. It's like a kind of light has gone out of my life. One I didn't even realize had been there.

I push back from the table in disgust. What am I thinking? I want her back in my bed, that's all. There are no finer feelings in the heart of Dante Bellanti, and there never will be. I can't afford that luxury. Or that weakness.

As I stalk down the hall and make my way upstairs toward my rooms, I mull over the current issue with the Abbott vines. We can't afford to lose them. The Abbott-Bellanti chianti is already presold for a thousand bottles.

Not only that, but we did a big thing by combining the wineries. Something like this hasn't been done before around here, and it's made quite a splash in the press. Everyone is talking about it. There's no way I can drop the ball now. What would people think if they find out that my winery can't make a claim on a single Abbott grape? My brothers and I have worked too hard to let a bunch of gossip stain the Bellanti Vineyards name.

Which is why I need to focus on business. Not my dick.

Taking out my phone, I pull up Frankie's contact, but then hesitate with my thumb over her name. It's late. She's probably in bed with her husband right now. All that warmth going to someone else. All that passion, wasted on a lowlife like Rico. Just thinking about it makes me cringe. A man like him doesn't know what to do with a woman like her.

Pacing the room, I realize I should've pressed Armani a little more deeply about his plans for Rico. I need to know what we're up against, and what our options are. Beyond Armani, we have an entire team of lawyers at our beck and call, but Rico knows he's got us over a barrel. I doubt he'd be interested in simply selling to us. Not for any reasonable price, that is.

But Frankie can be reasonable. I just don't know that she will be...fuck.

I detest texting, but for reasons I am not willing to examine at the moment, I can't quite stomach the thought of hearing her voice right now.

For the first time, I tap out a text to Frankie.

Meeting tomorrow morning. We need to settle this once and for all.

Then I hit send and power down my phone without waiting for a response. I know it's the only way I'll be able to sleep tonight—otherwise I'll be checking for her reply every five minutes.

I take a hot shower and then climb into bed, telling myself I'll deal with Frankie in the morning.

FRANKIE

"He's ruined everything else. He doesn't get to ruin my senior year, too."

I'm driving Livvie to Napa High, even though Charlie and I told our little sister she could skip school if she wanted. We thought a break might give her some time to deal with everything that's been going on, and there are only a few weeks left until winter vacation anyway. But Livvie was adamant. She said she didn't want to miss any of the reviews before midterm exams, insisting she'd finish the quarter with her usual straight As, come hell or high water.

It's about an hour and ten minutes to NHS, so we left extra early and hit the Starbucks drive thru before hitting the road this morning. Our breakfast sandwiches are long gone, though Livvie ate half of mine, but my little sister is still fiddling with the cardboard sleeve on her cup while she stares out the car window.

Even though she's tried her best to put on a happy

face, it's obvious that everything is weighing heavily on her—and I hate that I don't know how to make it better. I still see red every time I mentally replay that horrible scene with the men who came to the winery to take the Friesians. Which Dad still hasn't apologized for.

In fact, he hasn't reached out at all. Of course he hasn't. Slow clap for Absentee Father of the Year.

It's infuriating the way he's left Livvie without a positive male influence in her life. I know how I felt growing up without one. And look what happened—I eloped with the first man who threw any attention at me, married him without a second thought. His bullshit promises to take care of me were like my own personal aphrodisiac. I don't want that for my sister.

Unfortunately, solid father figures don't exactly fall from the sky when you need them.

Although...now that I think about it, I might know someone who fits the bill.

After I drop Livvie off at the school's front doors, I watch her disappear into the teeming rush of teenagers and overstuffed backpacks, and then go park in the lot.

It's been years since I walked these halls, and I can't help but smile as I make my way to the front office. School was my sanctuary, though I never fully appreciated that until after I'd graduated.

When I ask the admin behind the curved reception desk if I can visit Mr. Matthews, my old school counselor, she smiles. "Mr. Matthews is no longer a counselor here," she says.

"Oh," I say, deflating. "Do you know if he transferred somewhere else, or—"

"He is Vice Principal Matthews now," she clarifies. "And I happen to know that he's free."

She has me sign in on a clipboard and then motions me down the hall. As I knock on his door, I briefly wonder if he'll remember me. I'm sure he's seen thousands of students pass through NHS during his time here.

"Come on in," he calls out. Just the sound of his voice is a comfort.

When I step into his office, a welcoming smile spreads across his face.

"Hello."

"Francesca Abbott. What a nice surprise."

"You remember me," I say, pleased.

"How could I forget? You might be the only student I've ever had who never ducked into my office as an excuse to cut class," he teases.

Mr. Matthews is an older man with dark skin and warm brown eyes, though he has a lot more grey at his temples than he used to. He was always a steady presence when I went to school here, and though I hadn't visited him often—usually just to choose my electives or get my class schedules in order—I can honestly say that I've never felt as comfortable with any other man.

He gestures for me to take the seat across from him. "So. What can I do for you, Frankie?"

Haltingly, I remind him of how he'd reached out to me when I was a student at NHS. "I guess you'd surmised that things...weren't so easy at home. And you offered counseling. You also said I could stop by any time if I needed a break from class."

Nodding, he says, "My door's always open. That goes for all the kids here, even the ones who aren't on my roster. Although everyone's on my roster now."

"Congratulations on the promotion, by the way," I tell him.

"Thank you."

I lean forward. "So here's the thing...I didn't take you up on your offer at the time, but I realize now that I should have taken the help."

"No hard feelings," he says kindly. "Looks like you've turned out just fine."

"Yeah. But I guess I was just wondering..." It takes me a second to gather my thoughts, and my courage. "I'm wondering if I might be able to take you up on your offer now. Only not for myself, but for my sister."

"Olivia Abbott. Great student, great attitude. What's going on?"

The sincerity in his eyes makes me feel more confident, and I explain a little bit about our situation—not the worst of it, of course, but enough to give him an idea of what Livvie's going through.

"Maybe you could look out for her?" I ask. "Let her know...you know. That you're here. That she has someone she can talk to."

He spreads his hands. "Of course. I'm happy to help, however I can."

"She could use a good male influence, Mr. Matthews.

She needs to see...what that's like. I didn't have any good men in my life, and it's—I've made some choices I regret. I don't want Livvie to end up like me or Charlie."

His expression gets more serious. "Is she safe?"

"Yes. She's living with our older sister. Indefinitely. It's just been an adjustment."

"Okay. Good, then. I'll reach out to her this week." He pauses, seeming to mull something over. "You know, I can still help you, too, Frankie. If you want."

I laugh. "I appreciate that, Mr. Matthews. But my fate is sealed. It's too late for me."

Deep lines mar his forehead as he looks at me. "Any life can be changed. It's never too late."

I wave him off. "Livvie's the important one. What I've done, I've done for her. Please. Help her."

He reaches across the desk and lightly pats my hand. "I will. I promise you that. And I appreciate you dropping in to visit me—always good to see my old students again. Stop by any time."

I thank him again and leave, feeling marginally better for the first time in a long time. If only the nervous rolling in my stomach would stop.

Ever since I got Dante's text last night, my stomach's been a pit of nauseous dread. I assume that settling things "once and for all" means he's ready to serve me legal paperwork nullifying our marriage, or maybe he's found some loophole he can use to assert his claim on the Abbott Winery. Whatever he has in mind, it can't be good. I spend the short drive over to Bellanti Vineyards trying to calm myself down, and failing utterly.

I'm leaning against the parked car staring at the door to the Bellanti offices (and gathering my courage to go inside) when I spot Candi coming out of the tasting room.

She smiles, looking like she wants to talk, but I wave her off with a friendly smile of my own, starting resolutely down the gravel drive toward the offices. I'm afraid if I stop for chitchat, I'm going to completely lose my nerve.

But Candi doesn't get the hint and hurries over to intercept me before I reach the door.

"Frankie! It's so good to see you." She throws her arms around me in a bear hug that almost has me breaking down. Lowering her voice, she adds, "Are you on your way to see Dante, by any chance?"

"Actually, yes. Why? Did you need something from him? Because I don't think I'm the best person to be asking him for any favors right now—"

"No, no. Not at all. I just...look, I don't know exactly what's going on, but I know it's not good. Which is none of my business, and that's okay, but I thought I should give you a heads-up that Dante's been a beast for the past few days according to the staff."

"So what else is new?" I quip.

"Seriously," Candi commiserates. "But yeah. I was supposed to meet with him a half hour ago, but he never showed. Apparently he left the office in a rush earlier and never came back. Said he had to take care of something at the house."

"That's weird. And rude, considering you had a meeting scheduled with him."

Candi shrugs. "Too bad, I had to meet with Armani instead..."

"Doesn't seem like you were too put out," I say, picking up on her dreamy look.

"Do not get me started," she says. "I could meet with Armani Bellanti all day long. That man isn't just eye candy—he's the entire candy store. Perfection."

With that, she gives her fingers the classic chef's kiss, and I can't help laughing along with her.

"Okay, well, thanks for the intel," I say, feeling a little less panicked thanks to Candi's sassiness. "I'd better go find him before he disappears off to somewhere else."

After a few more words of encouragement and another hug, she heads to her car. I take a deep, steadying breath and then turn on my heel and take the path toward the main house.

The front door is locked, which is odd—it's the first time I've ever encountered that during the day—so I go around to the back door. Hopefully Alain will let me in if he's working in the kitchen. I'm just about to check the door handle when I hear a faint voice speaking in Italian from an open window somewhere. Huh.

I follow the sound around the other side of the house, until I'm close enough to the window to catch the sound of the deep male voice culminating in a, *"Bellissima,* Jessica."

It's like I'm compelled to stand on my tiptoes and peer over the sill, and it only takes half a second's glance to see my nemesis on her knees across the room. She sits back and licks her lips like a satisfied cat. She's practically purring.

My throat burns with bile. I've been nauseous with worry all morning, and now I'm flooded with a sickening rage that pushes me over the edge. I bolt for the hedges that line the walkway and lose what little breakfast I had into the bushes.

I'm shaking all over as I stalk back to the car. God *damn* him. Right to hell. And damn me for feeling this way. I'm the married one, after all. Dante doesn't owe his loyalty to anyone. Fuck, fuck, fuck these stupid feelings.

I get in the car and slam the door, then slump down in the driver's seat, hands over my face. I can't do this.

I dig my phone out of my bag and send Dante a text.

My husband and I will meet with you tomorrow morning to discuss the terms of our arrangement. 9 a.m. We'll finish everything.

16

FRANKIE

RICO IS in the passenger seat, tapping an excited drum-beat on the dash with his fingers. Mere inches away, I'm trying my best not to kill him. I don't know what I ever saw in this asshole.

I picked him up in Vallejo on my way north from San Francisco, and now I have to drop Livvie off at school. After that, Rico and I will go see Dante at the Bellanti offices. That is, if I don't strangle Rico first.

I glance in the rearview mirror at Livvie in the back seat. She's staring out the window, headphones in, a slight crease between her brows as she pretends to ignore me and Rico. God, I never wanted these two parts of my world to meet.

Yet seeing my precious little sister and the scumbag I married sitting in a car together only steels my resolve further. I remind myself that Rico Correa is an inconvenience that I need to get around. Livvie, on the other hand, is what really matters—even if it means losing something to Rico.

Tossing and turning in bed last night, I mulled over my (admittedly limited) options. In the end, I decided it made the most sense to just get as much for the vineyard as I can from the Bellantis, dump half the profits on Rico, and then tell him I never want to see him again. With any luck, the money will be enough to get him to sign divorce papers and go back to Italy without a fight. He sure as hell won't agree to a divorce before he lines his pockets, I know that much. I just wish there was another way out of this.

It kills me to think about selling the vineyard, but my sisters and I are survivors. We can do a pretty decent amount of surviving with a couple million dollars. I know the vineyard is worth at least that, and the Bellantis know it, too. Especially since I've already proven the viability of combining our grapes, given the popularity of the upcoming blended chianti. So that's that. It is what it is. Family heritage is one thing, but living family members is something immeasurably more important.

And if the Bellantis are going to make a mint off my family's property, the least they can do is compensate us fairly. Even if Dante's an asshole about it, I have to believe he'll be fair in the end. Armani will urge him to do the right thing, and I'm pretty sure Marco will, too.

We pull up to the curb at Napa High and drop Livvie off. She leans forward between the seats and says, "Thanks, Frankie. And good luck with your meeting."

"I'm gonna need it," I tell her, dropping a quick kiss on the top of her head.

Her door barely shuts before Rico starts talking.

"So. Let's go over my plan." He makes a final drum-roll with his fingers on the dash and ends with a flourish of air guitar. "I have it all figured out."

I grip the wheel tighter as I pull out of the parking lot. "Okay..."

"We need to present a united front, you see. Convince the Bellantis that we have decided to make a go of the winery. If they think we are not willing to let go, it will drive up the price."

The thought of playing the happy wife with Rico has zero appeal to me.

"Why don't we just put an offer on the table and say we're firm on it?" I suggest.

Rico looks over with a frown. "Frankie. We have to play hard to get. The more we resist selling, the higher the price will go. Can you imagine what they might offer if they think we are going to keep it? They would not just be losing the vines, they would have a rival next door."

"You're right," I say. I hate that I agree with him on this.

The Bellantis have already invested quite a bit in the Abbott vineyards. Not only that, but rolling out the specialty blend from our mutual grapes was very costly. Canceling all those orders might be committing retail suicide with the vendors, not to mention destroying all the goodwill that's been built up. And Armani would have a public relations nightmare on his hands.

"I will do all the talking," Rico says smoothly.

"We're fifty-fifty owners," I remind him, annoyed. "Plus, I know Dante a lot better than you do. He's not the kind of man who—"

"I know what kind of man he is. He will appreciate talking *da uomo a uomo*."

Man to man. Right. I roll my eyes at the expression. Rico just grins beside me.

Minutes later, I turn into the gates of the Bellanti estate. I pass the offices and continue down the drive to the main house. I'm hoping it's far enough away from the eyes of curious employees...and malicious ones named Jessica.

I park on the side of the house and quickly get out of the car, taking a deep breath to steady myself. Rico goes on ahead, as if he knows exactly where he's going. I used to think his swagger indicated confidence. Now I just think it makes him look like a dumbass.

"Wrong door, Rico. That's the kitchen," I call to him. "Follow me."

Gesturing to the front door, I walk over without waiting for him. When I ring the bell, the door opens with a welcoming smile from the housekeeper that falters a bit at the sight of Rico. I pause just over the threshold and smooth my hands over my pencil skirt and fitted jacket, which I'm wearing with a light blue blouse beneath. My outfit doesn't scream wealth the way it did when I was a Bellanti, but it's the best I could do and I'm going to own it.

"Nice place," Rico says. The housekeeper just nods.

We're shown down the hall, to the dining room. Everyone else is already gathered there and waiting— Marco, Dante, and Armani seated on one side of the table and goddamned Jessica standing behind Dante with her tablet poised to take notes.

Dante's eyes sweep over me, dark and impassive. I'm glad I can't read his mind. I can only imagine what's going through his head as his gaze turns to Rico.

Armani clears his throat and gestures at the empty chairs on the other side of the table. "Please, take a seat. Coffee?"

"No thank you," I murmur at the same time Rico says, "Of course."

Alain appears out of nowhere and deposits a steaming cup in front of Rico, who takes his sweet time mixing in cream and sugar while everybody waits for him to finish clanging his spoon around in the cup. He takes a long slurp, and I try not to squirm in my seat. I've never felt so awkward.

"I would like to get right to the point," Rico announces, setting his cup down. "We have decided we are keeping the winery."

Armani flicks an eyebrow. "You're...*keeping* the winery." It's obvious he's shocked.

Rico leans back in his chair. I almost expect him to kick back and cross his ankles on the tabletop. "We have it all planned out. We will fill all the outstanding orders right away, then have the grapes picked, get them pressed, and start expanding promotions to get more sales."

It's taking everything in me to not cringe. When it

comes to vinification, or even simply running a business, Rico has no idea what he's talking about, and it's obvious.

He's completely ignorant about choosing the right grapes, primary and secondary fermentation, racking, aging, and blending. Even if it were possible to rush Abbott grapes to pressing right away, good wine takes time—and great wine takes longer. I wouldn't expect Abbott wines to be available in any kind of saleable quantity for eighteen months, minimum.

Before Rico can go on further about his "big plans" for the Abbott Winery, Dante smooths his tie and says, "Unfortunately, you can't fill any outstanding orders without inventory—which the Abbotts don't have at the moment. It's also a bit late in the season to harvest as many grapes as you'd need to fill all those orders. Not to mention, Bellanti Vineyards has already harvested a good portion of the crop. I doubt you'll have a decent wine for...oh, I'd say eighteen to twenty-four months. Though I suppose you could fill your backorders then. Assuming the wine turns out well enough.

"But I doubt the vendors will still be interested in your wine by then—or now, even. If anything, they'd probably prefer refunds over having their backorders fulfilled. Of course, you'll have to get them to talk to you first, which will be...a challenge. The Abbott name isn't worth much around these parts, thanks to the way your father-in-law ran his business."

Dante's cold tirade is hitting me like a knife in the gut, but every word of it is true.

Rico's smile persists. "We will rename the winery, of course! Simple."

I press my fingers to my temples and close my eyes. Dante and Marco chuckle quietly across the table, but it's loud in my ears. We've been here all of five minutes and Rico is already fucking this up. I have to do something, fast. Steer the conversation back in the right direction.

"What Mr. Correa *means to say*," I cut in, "is that we intend to begin production as soon as it's feasible again. Sadly, yes, the purchase orders my father took on good faith will not be filled this season because the wine is not available. But we intend to—"

"The exact timing does not matter," Rico interrupts, dismissing me with a wave of his hand. "We intend to move forward with *our* winery. Right, *cara?*"

Rico has never called me "dear" before, and I find it nauseating. "Well, yes, but first we'll have to—" I start.

"With all these plans that we have, it would take a lot to convince us to turn over our business to someone else and simply walk away," Rico says, interrupting me again. He turns his head to look in Dante's direction. "And by a lot, I mean *a lot.*"

It's tacky and not at all subtle, the way Rico is trying to get Dante to start throwing out numbers. It's also not going to work. Rico's just blown our plan out of the water.

We should have done this my way from the start. Walked in here, told the Bellantis how much we'd take for the vineyard, explained that we were firm on it, and negotiated the whole thing in minutes. Instead, we're stuck putting on this idiotic charade.

I'm fucking done with it.

"Look. I'm honestly not interested in playing games," I try again. "It seems like it would be most beneficial to all of us to try to get a purchase agreement for the Abbott compound on the table before we leave today. Now, given that prime acreage in Napa goes for about three to four hundred thousand per acre, on average, I think it would be fair to start—"

"My wife is speaking out of turn," Rico says. "We do not wish to sell."

"Actually," I say, trying to remain calm, "as an equal stakeholder in the property—"

Suddenly, Rico pushes me back from the table with his palm against my chest. His fingers end up splayed across my breast, but rather than move his hand away, he takes the opportunity to grope me instead. It's so unexpected and inappropriate that all I can do is sit there, frozen, a fake smile pasted on my face. Inside, I'm screaming.

But then I see the fury in Dante's eyes. It's enough to spur me to action.

Clearing my throat, I remove Rico's hand. This meeting has gone to hell, and I'm afraid that no matter what I say, Rico is going to gloss right over me.

"Okay." I put my palms down on the table. "Can we please take five minutes?"

Dante hasn't taken his eyes off me this entire time, but he remains silent. Armani nods toward the door.

I get up as gracefully as I can, while Rico looks at me

questioningly from his seat. I tilt my head toward the hallway, indicating that he needs to follow me.

Out in the hall, I take a few deep breaths, trying to steady my stomach again. Rico comes up behind me moments later, as excited as a puppy who doesn't understand when he's done something wrong.

"We're going to be millionaires!" He grabs my shoulders, massaging me as he talks, clearly turned on by how rich he thinks he's about to be. "We are so close!"

"Rico," I whisper. "You need to slow down in there. You don't know what you're talking about. You can't produce wine on a whim. It takes months to years to produce a quality bottle. You need to let me take the reins on this."

"You want to know what you need to let *me* do?"

He runs his hands from my shoulders up to my neck and then back down, getting handsier by the second. Stepping into me, Rico presses his chest against mine. The wall is behind my back and there's nowhere for me to go. He starts leaning in for a kiss that I can't possibly avoid.

When Rico's lips land on mine, I push back my disgust and tolerate it for a second or two (in case the Bellantis are watching from the other room) before I twist my face away. "Okay, that's enough. We should go back in."

"We were just getting started," he says with a smile.

Sidestepping him, I straighten my suit jacket. "Like I said, let me do the talking."

I get about two steps away before Rico grabs my arm.

"Rico—"

The next thing I know, he's flinging me into the living room and pushing me against the wall, his tongue slithering around my mouth like it has a mind of its own. I wriggle in his grasp but he gets even rougher, biting my lip and sticking his hand up my skirt.

"What are you doing?" I manage to choke out.

"I want to fuck you right here, in the Bellantis' house. We need to celebrate, baby."

I try to twist away, but it's futile.

"*Stop*," I tell him, as loud as I dare. I don't want anyone to overhear us, but I'm not going to let Rico just paw at me. "Get *off*."

"I'm planning on it," he whispers gleefully, squeezing my ass painfully hard through my underwear. "Come on, Frankie. Just a quickie."

"No. Let me go. Now." I pummel my fists against his chest and hiss, "*I said no!*"

He presses his torso into me, pinning me in place as he tugs my skirt up my thighs.

"You used to love my cock," he's saying. "Don't you remember?"

My stomach convulses as I attempt one last time, with all my might, to push him away. But he's too tall, too strong, and he seems to have completely lost any common sense. He's running on pure lust, high on a power trip. There's nothing I can do to stop him.

"Stop, Rico, dammit! Stop—"

Suddenly, his body goes flying backwards. I hear him hit the floor, but all I see is Dante, standing there with his fists clenched at his sides, his chest heaving with hard breaths. Armani and Marco are behind him. All of the Bellanti brothers look ready to crack some skulls.

Rico scrambles to his feet, but doesn't have a chance to get his bearings before Dante pushes him back, farther away from me.

"She said no," Dante growls.

"She's my wife," Rico says, a shit-eating grin on his face. "She *belongs* to me. I can do with her what I want."

Dante moves so his body is between me and Rico, blocking my view. Dante's voice drops to a quiet, murderous rumble that I've never heard from him before.

"She told you no," he says slowly. "You *don't touch her* when she says no. Now get the fuck out of my house."

Rico laughs, but it comes out weakly. "You can't do anything to me, I'm—"

He's cut off by Armani and Marco grabbing him. Taking an arm each, they march him out the door, leaving me and Dante in sudden silence.

17

DANTE

Frankie's eyes are glassy with shock, her lips pressed into a tight line as she slumps against the wall.

I still can't believe that asshole laid his hands on her, and right in my own fucking home.

"You don't belong to him," I tell her.

Approaching slowly, I reach out and cup the side of her face, moving my thumb over her soft skin. I want nothing more than to gather her up in my arms and comfort her, but I'm afraid to. Seeing Correa overpower her like that...it puts some of my past actions in a whole new light.

We had discussed it once, sort of, but seeing the fear that Correa put into her eyes makes me feel sick. Frankie won't even look at me. Her eyes are on the floor, her body trembling, as if she's still caught between fight and flight.

"What he did...when he touched you like that..." I trail off, shaking my head. "Have I done that? I just...did I ever make you—"

She finally looks up at me. "I always wanted you, Dante. Every single time."

With a rush of relief, I give in to my caveman impulses and pull her into my arms. She belongs to me, not that asshole, regardless of what any marriage certificate says. I inhale her scent, gently stroke her hair. I've spent all this time trying to get her out of my head, trying to pretend I didn't want her, shoving back my feelings, acting like I have the same heart of stone my father did. But the truth is, I've missed her more than I could ever put into words.

I'm done fighting it.

Her body is tense in my arms but she slowly relaxes by degrees. The hard rise and fall of her chest eventually slows, and then she's melting against me, her cheek pressed into my chest. Her hands gripping the lapels of my jacket.

I pull back to tip her chin up and press my lips softly to hers. Just for a moment, just long enough to reassure her, with zero aggression in case she doesn't want this. In fact, I'm almost expecting her to push me away.

Instead, her arms wrap around me as she sinks into the kiss, opening her mouth wider, stroking my tongue hungrily with hers. Now that I've had a hit, I can't stop tasting her, drinking her in. My tongue runs along hers, hot and heavy, my body pressing her against the wall. Until suddenly her hands move to my chest, cutting through the cloud of lust as she pushes me away.

I back up with a pant. The pain in her eyes brings back some of my uneasiness.

"I'm sorry," I murmur. "I didn't mean to—"

"It's not that. I just...I can't do this, Dante. I can't hop in and out of your bed, not when I know I'm not the only one there. I know you're with Jessica. And fuck if my self-esteem isn't a complete joke at this point, but—"

"I'm not with Jessica," I blurt. "I brought her back because..."

Because I'd wanted to make Frankie jealous. But now I can see how petty, how beneath me a move like that had been. How goddamned manipulative it was.

"...because?" Frankie prods.

"Because I needed help," I finish. "You made so many changes—good changes—that I got overwhelmed. I've never really been the hands-on type with our employees the way you are, and as for managing inventory...I basically see it as a hassle and a chore."

I'm a little surprised to realize that I'm telling the truth.

Looking into her eyes, I lay it all out. "I need you to come back to the winery. I need you in every aspect of my life." I reach out for her once more, and she steps into my embrace. Nothing has ever felt more right. "Please, Frankie."

Oh God, I'm really begging her.

"Please what?" she asks, still questioning it. And how could she not, after how I've treated her?

"Please..." I take a deep breath, my heart and mind at war, my sky-high, ironclad defensive walls battling the exact emotions I've spent my whole life working to hide, to bury, to deny. "Please let me love you," I finally say, my arms wrapped tight around her. "I love you."

Frankie puts a hand on my cheek, gazing up at me. Silently, she pulls out of my arms, and for just a moment I feel my world tilt sideways. She's going to walk away, once and for all.

But then she takes my hand and leads me from the room, down the hall, to the staircase. Up the stairs, and into my bedroom. The second the door closes behind us, I swing her into my arms, melting at the sensation of her warm hand looping around the back of my neck. I can barely believe this is happening as I carry her across the room and set her gently on my bed.

"Tell me you want this," I say, searching her eyes.

Solemnly, she says, "I want this. I want *you*."

I kiss her as slowly as I can while stripping off her jacket and working at the front of her blouse, undoing one tiny button at a time. I don't think I've ever taken the time to properly unwrap her before. Maybe I could get used to this kind of anticipation.

The zipper on her skirt comes down, the fabric easing over her thighs. My lips cruise her neck, her chest, her cleavage as I tug the blouse over her head, my nails skimming along her ribs when I reach behind her to unfasten her bra and slide it down her arms. I can't stop kissing her, touching her, my lips and fingers seemingly registering her for the first time all over again.

She threads her fingers into my hair as we kiss. I see soft acceptance and heady eagerness in her eyes when I briefly pull away to undress. I had thought that angry, fiery Frankie was the best version of sex—but this completely willing, completely open Frankie is another level.

She holds her arms out to me as I settle between her open thighs and kiss the warm spot between her full, magnificent breasts. Then I take my time to lap and tug at her swollen nipples while cradling her breasts in my palms. The taste of her, sweet in my mouth, is like nothing else on earth.

"Dante." My name drips from her mouth as she opens her legs and tips her hips, welcoming me.

I want to sink into her, but I'm not ready yet. Kissing my way down her body, I explore between her legs with my fingers. Parting her, tracing her delicate lips, making her gasp and squirm with need. I lower my mouth to taste her, my tongue skimming every seductive rise. Her breasts rise so perfectly as she arches her back while I lick her clit.

She tugs at me, moaning my name, urging me to move up and over her body. Then her hands wrap around my ass and she pulls me close, guiding me into her.

I sink right in, my cock as straight and true as an arrow finding its target, a groan escaping my lips as I drown in the sensation. She's so wet, so fucking hot, and the way she's digging her nails into my skin I can tell she wants me deep inside her, every last inch of me. Holy. Shit. I thrust carefully, afraid the potent pleasure is going to push me over the edge right away.

Her hips meet my every thrust, her soft, wet heat stroking me so good I feel like I'm losing my mind.

"Yes," I breathe, gliding in and out, long and slow and so agonizingly gentle. "Yes, fuck, Frankie, yes."

"You feel so good to me," she pants.

"You're perfect," I tell her.

She slides her hands around to my hips, skimming them up my chest, around the back of my neck. She's breathing even harder now, despite my slow pace—or maybe because of it.

"Dante," she whispers. "Look at me."

I obey, my eyes meeting hers, and immediately I feel her core start to clench around my cock, the orgasm taking hold of her. I can tell she's coming hard, blinking rapidly as tears fill her eyes, her mouth falling open as she gasps for air. But she doesn't look away from me.

"I love you," she tells me breathlessly.

I feel a warmth, a connection wash over me. Something I've never had before. This is what it's supposed to be like. This is how love is supposed to be.

And suddenly I'm coming with her, spilling into her helplessly as I whisper my love right back. We're coming together now, oh God, oh *fucking* God, yes, and with every thrust it's like I'm pouring my entire soul into her for safekeeping. My body is shuddering. I've never come so hard in my fucking life.

I hold her close in the comedown, rolling onto my back and pulling her on top of me, still needing to be skin to skin without crushing her delicate body. I can feel her heart beating against mine as we ride out the last lingering aftershocks.

Closing my eyes, I softly kiss the top of her head and settle in, my whole body relaxed.

The rise and fall of her breathing evens out, growing slower and steadier, and within a few minutes it's obvious that she's fallen asleep. I lightly run my fingers up and down her back, relishing the feel of her skin. It's funny to think about it, but I'd only been vaguely aware of the existence of the Abbott sisters before my marriage to Frankie was contracted.

Everyone in wine country is somewhat familiar with other people in the industry, of course, the large wineries especially. But beyond that mild, passing familiarity with her, all I'd really known about Francesca Abbott was that her father had been deeply in debt to mine.

The realization hits me that I still know very little about the woman sleeping in my arms. I did have Armani run a background check on her, but I stopped short of getting a full dossier worked up. Normally, my brother does what I like to call "opposition research," so I know exactly what I'm up against. But Frankie isn't some opponent to be conquered. I see that now.

I guess my father taught me and my brothers to see anybody without the Bellanti name as a potential enemy. But ever since my father's death, it's become even more important to me to be less like my father—and it's time to stop letting his cynical view of the world shape mine.

My father's way of living got him murdered, after all. And I don't want that.

Though I'd be more than happy to stay in bed for the rest of the day, I know Frankie and I both have responsibilities to get back to, so I gently kiss her awake. She looks at me through sleepy eyes and flashes me a lazy smile.

"Let's go away for a little while. Just the weekend, just you and me."

"Are you kidding? Dante Bellanti wants to take a vacation?" she asks, a teasing lilt in her voice. "I don't believe it."

"You still have clothes here—you can pack a bag and we could leave here in an hour."

"I can't." She sits up and shakes her head, smiling. "I mean, I'd love to, but I drove here in Charlie's car, and I still have to take Livvie back to Nob Hill after she gets out of school."

"Fine with me," I say. "We can fly out of SFO. Just go to ticketing at the airport and buy a trip to anywhere we want."

She just laughs good-naturedly and slides off the bed, looking around on the floor for her clothes. As she starts to get dressed, I have to fight the flicker of panic going through me.

"Please..." That word is so unfamiliar on my tongue. And yet I can't seem to quit saying it today.

She pulls her shirt over her head and her skirt over her hips. Buttoning the blouse, she turns to look at me. "I'm going to pick up Livvie in a bit. Then I'm going to take her home to Nob Hill."

"Frankie—"

"And then I'm going to meet you at the St. Regis, and we're going to spend the night making up for lost time. In their most luxurious suite. And yes, they have room service."

I lay there and watch her finish getting dressed because honestly, I can't bring myself to move. She's mesmerizing me. Her words make me feel warm, excited, and anxious to be with her again. She pulls me in for a kiss before she leaves my room.

"See you soon," she says.

The door shuts behind her and I realize that I'm actually smiling for the first time in far too long.

I'm really, truly smiling.

18

FRANKIE

When I enter the opulent lobby of the St. Regis Hotel, I see Dante waiting for me.

There are gleaming parquet floors, stately floral arrangements, and crystal light fixtures galore, but I only have eyes for him as he rises from a wingback chair and crosses the room.

This might be the first time I've seen him dressed semi-casually, with the top few buttons of his dress shirt undone and the sleeves rolled up, accentuating his muscular forearms. No tie, no jacket. It's sexy as hell.

He immediately takes my hand and pulls me in for a kiss. My heart flutters at the feel of his lips. It's like kissing him for the first time all over again, but a different version of him. One who actually loves me.

"I'm sorry to say that we won't be in the best suite tonight," he says.

"Oh no," I say with mock horror.

"Apparently there's a visiting dignitary residing in the

Presidential for the month, so we've been accommodated in the St. Regis Suite. Alas, it is only the second best."

"The nerve!" I grin and nudge him with my shoulder. "How *dare* international politics get in the way of our fuckfest."

Dante actually barks out a rough laugh. I can't help but grin. It sounds a little rusty. I made a silent vow to myself to help him get more practice at it.

He takes my small bag and my hand and leads me to the elevators. The car is empty when we step inside. The second the doors close, he pulls me in for a deep kiss. I let myself fall into him, savoring his lips, his tongue, the taste of him.

I'd been daydreaming of nothing but Dante ever since I left the Bellanti estate earlier to pick up Livvie from school and drive her back to Charlie's. My little sister caught on to my changed mood immediately and eyed me suspiciously, but the only comment she'd made was to wonder out loud what had happened to Rico. When I shrugged, she didn't push further.

Charlie was understandably interested in how the meeting at Bellanti Vineyards had gone, but I simply said that we were still working on negotiations—and that I'd be spending the weekend with Dante. That earned me a few raised brows, but when Livvie hugged me goodbye, she'd whispered, "Good luck," in my ear.

I wasn't just being coy—I didn't want to give my sisters false hope about what was going to happen to our winery. And I also needed to see how things went with me and Dante before I made any final decisions.

With a ding, the elevator opens onto a wide hallway. The colors soothing and neutral, with baroque gold mirrors and matching sconces spaced out along the walls. Dante leads the way to our room, swipes the key card, and pushes open the door.

Soft light fills the space as we drop our things in the marble entry and step into the posh room. The first thing I notice is the wall of windows in the living area, which offers a stunning view of downtown San Francisco. The city is lit up in all its brilliance, so close it looks like you could reach out and touch it. There are even a few stars twinkling in the sky.

I press my hands against the glass and drink in the view. "Dante, you need to see—"

But he's already there, right behind me, wrapping his arms around my waist. His cheek presses against the side of my head and he whispers in my ear.

"It's a beautiful view."

I nod and relax into his embrace. There's no urgency right now. This is our time—time to be together. To be close. We've never done this before, but I'm glad we are now. He finally pulls away and gives me a kiss on top of my head. "I'll put our things in the bedroom."

I watch his tight ass as he walks away. I'm tempted to follow him, but I take a quick look around instead. The walls are done in a soothing shade of lavender that brings a smile to my face. There's a textured cream rug over the dark wood floors and sleekly modern furniture uphol-stered in shades of natural and merlot linen. I move from the sitting room into the bedroom. A massive bed sits in the center flanked by marble-topped end tables. Artwork with an equestrian theme graces the walls, and a plush chaise nestles against a pair of arched windows that look out toward the water. My eyes are drawn again to the bed. Dante catches me looking.

"Hungry?" He arches a brow.

"Starved," I say suggestively, grabbing his ass with a little squeeze.

He cracks a smile, almost laughing again at my corny joke. "I'll order room service."

We end up eating on the couch, sharing a light supper of scallops with roasted squash, parsnip puree, and wild rice as we take in the city lights and talk.

"This is nice," Dante says, gesturing between us. "Ever since I can remember, we had to eat all our dinners at that long-ass formal dining table. Seven sharp, every night. If you were late, the door would be locked and you'd have to go to bed without a scrap."

"Jesus," I murmur.

"Dad didn't believe in having conversations while eating, either," he adds. "Said it was low class. Rude. So it was usually dead silent. Not to mention all the other rules he enforced. Elbows off the table, both feet flat on the floor, napkin in lap, use the correct fork...all that shit."

"Wow." I had noticed that Dante and his younger brothers weren't big talkers at the table, but I assumed it was just personal preference. Not something that had been drilled in them.

"Yeah," he goes on. "It wasn't so bad when my mom and sister were there, but after we lost them...it was down to just my brothers and our dad. Dinner always felt like a last meal, you know? Though I guess we all got impeccable table manners out of it. How about your family?"

I have to think back to remember what it was like having dinner as a family at our house.

"My mom...walked out on us when we were little," I tell him slowly. "So it was just my sisters and our dad, too. Except he wasn't around for dinner all that often, and when he was, he was usually under the influence."

"I'm sorry," Dante says. "I'm prying. I shouldn't have—"

"No, no, it's fine. Dad had to eat too, so he'd leave a little grocery money out for us every week. We actually— my sisters and I—would take turns cooking. If it wasn't too cold outside, we'd eat on the back porch together. It was nice. Even on the nights we had to eat cereal and toast, I wouldn't have wished it any other way."

I smile at the memories, and tell Dante about the disastrous time Charlie tried to cook her first Thanksgiving turkey and the fire department had shown up because we couldn't get the smoke alarm to go off.

"Unfortunately," I continue, "we had put the smoking roasting pan on the back porch, and while the firemen were giving us a stern talking-to, our yellow Lab, Penny, snuck out and started eating the blackened thing."

"Oh no. Was she okay?"

"Yeah. But we were so freaked out that she'd end up with turkey bone splinters in her stomach that we rushed her to the ER vet for x-rays. She was absolutely fine, thank God."

I finish up the story for Dante, because it has the best ending.

Dragging ourselves home late that night, we had stopped off at the Alvarez fruit stand to see if we could get some kind of food wrapped up to go, but Delores ushered us all inside and plated up hearty servings of their leftovers so my sisters and I—and our dog—could eat together in her warm, cozy kitchen.

By the time I'm done, Dante is grinning from ear to ear. We talk carefully about our childhoods some more, swapping stories about how we grew up. Some are good, but many are not. This is a door I've never stepped through with him. With anyone, really, besides my sisters.

I open up about some of the things Charlie and I have done to protect Livvie from our dad, and how closely bonded the three of us are because of him. I don't bring up the marriage he forced on me, though. My truce with Dante is still too new, and I feel like it needs protecting.

"I guess we both had pretty fucked-up fathers," Dante muses.

He talks about his mom and his sister, who disappeared at sea when he was a teenager. About how it changed his father, made him more suspicious—and much more vicious as well. He talks about the discipline Enzo had insisted on, in every aspect of their lives.

"It made Armani a good soldier, but it had the opposite effect on Marco. He rebelled. Ran wild. He's starting to come around, but I don't know if he'll ever fully settle down," Dante says. "Lately he's been on this car racing kick. It's like he's legitimately addicted to danger."

"What about you?" I ask. "Did the discipline make you a good soldier, too?"

He goes quiet for a moment. "He made me like him. And I don't think I want to be. Not anymore."

"Then don't," I say simply.

I get up and put our empty dishes on the room service cart, then wheel it into the foyer and come back with both my hands out toward Dante.

"Come to bed," I tell him.

His expression is all seriousness as he takes my hands, rising from the couch, but as soon as I start undressing him in the bedroom his eyes grow dark with heat.

He's had so little comfort in his life. Hell, so have I, and I want us to find it together. As much as I want to take this slow, I'm increasingly needy and wanting as I strip him bare. I'm about to push him onto the bed, but he takes my wrist.

"Let me return the favor."

With that, he begins undressing me, taking his time. As my clothes come off, my gaze drops to his thick, hard cock. The sight of it has my mouth watering. The second my panties hit the floor, we tumble in a naked heap on the bed, not bothering to kick back the covers.

Dante covers me with his body, his lips finding my neck. I let my hands wander, touching him everywhere. Tracing the lines of his sculpted chest, the ridges of his abdomen.

When I grip his cock, he jerks with a little moan, hot precum running over my fingers.

"I wanted to go slow, but—"

"Anything you want, Frankie. Anything."

He leans down to kiss me, but I stop him with a finger on his lips. "You, inside me. Now."

Our eyes meet and he clasps my hands in his, our fingers interlocking as he dives into me with one hard, perfect thrust. For a moment we're both still, reveling in the feeling of our connection. When I'm ready, I swing my hips, urging him to plunge into me again, and he does. Faster and faster. We make love with our eyes open, finding once more that hard, driving tempo from this morning. But this time we're climbing the mountain together, instead of fighting it.

With every thrust I arch up to meet him, my nipples tingling against his chest, my center throbbing with pleasure. He rides me urgently, stroking that place within that makes me come in a hot rush every fucking time. Dante knows exactly what he's doing.

I hear his name rolling from my lips, drowning out the sound of our heavy breathing. The tempo is insane, the tension so tight that I could cry. The veins on the sides of his neck strain as he tenses, his cock swelling and growing even harder. Moving his hips, he changes position slightly so the base of him hits my clit, rolling over it with delicious friction. It's the kicker that I need. The tension snaps, floods, bursts apart, and I scream his name as I come apart.

I'm shaking, falling to pieces, his body wrapped in my

arms, and Dante groans his own completion, so deep inside that he feels like a part of me. His cock shudders in a hard spurt, and as I realize he's filling me with his hot seed, a second orgasmic wave ripples softly through me, taking my breath away.

We fall asleep in each other's arms.

My next conscious thought is how bright the sun is shining through my eyelids...and what the hell is that sound? I hear short grunts, heavy breathing. Fast. Rhythmic.

Supremely confused, I sit up quickly in bed, rubbing my eyes against the morning light. The ache between my legs jogs my memory, hard, and I look around the room for Dante.

I spot him on the floor beside the bed, doing push-ups in his boxer briefs. Judging by the gleam of sweat across his naked back, he's been at it for a while.

"Oh, you're working out," I say. "From the noise, I almost thought you were..."

"What?" he asks, without slowing his pace.

"I mean, you know..."

He looks up to shoot me a quick glance. I make a fist and pump it back and forth in the motion that all guys are very familiar with.

Dante pauses, then collapses onto the floor, facedown in the carpet. Alarmed, I lean over the side of the bed.

"Oh my God, are you okay?"

He rolls over, and I realize he's laughing. Hard, doubled over peals of laughter. I can't help but join him.

In one swift motion, he reaches up and drags me from the bed. I slide right off and land on top of him, both of us still giggling like children. My bare legs spread wide over his briefs, his cock perfectly palpable beneath the thin fabric. Dante stops laughing, his eyes doing that dark, lusty, serious thing again as they rake over my naked body.

Hitching a brow, it's my turn to take his wrists and wrench them above his head. "Keep them there. Or else."

He looks pleased at my mock seriousness. "Yes, ma'am."

Leaning forward, I position my breasts over his face, my nipples nearly touching his lips. He strains to take one in his mouth, but I pull back.

"No, no. You don't need to do anything. Just let me take care of you."

Reaching down, I grab the waistband of his boxers and tug them down until his cock springs free. Then I take his length in my hand, giving him three firm strokes.

"Frankie—"

"Shh..."

His eyes flutter closed and I sink down onto him, impaling myself to the hilt. He moves to touch me, but I quickly grab his forearms and pin him down again.

"Uh-uh. Nope. Be a good boy."

I toss my head and fling my hair over my shoulder, grinding on him, pressing kisses against his jaw, his neck, his chest, letting my breasts graze against him. Every time he tries to move his hands, I reassert my grip on his wrists.

"Never knew you could be so dominant in bed," Dante growls.

"There's a lot you don't know about me," I tease. "Yet."

Leaning back to take him more fully inside me, I tilt my head back and let my breasts bounce with every swing of my hips. I writhe and moan, knowing he's getting a million-dollar view of my pussy with his cock inside it. The thought turns me on even more. This is the sex goddess feeling I've been looking for. It's amazing to be in control...to take my pleasure this way, at my own pace, while he can do nothing but enjoy.

He watches as I reach down and slip a finger over my clit.

"Fuck," he groans. "Let me see you touch yourself."

His acceptance flames me on, and I continue to stroke myself while riding him. He sighs deeply, and I can feel the tension in his body start to relax. His fingers flex, and I know he's dying to touch me. With a smile, I finally release his forearms, placing one of his hands over my breast and the other on my cheek.

Working myself furiously, I grind on his cock and turn my face into his palm to kiss there, softly but hungrily. He groans again and again as I trail kisses along the sensitive inside of his wrist. My core starts to clench around him, and I know I can't hold back any longer.

I let loose a deep moan, and Dante whispers, "Yes," knowing what's about to happen.

When I come, I bring him with me, in a slow but powerful release that leaves us both trembling. Shattered and spent, I sprawl on top of him, scattering lazy kisses along his neck.

"See? Good things happen when you trust me," I murmur. "They might be different and new, but they're still good things."

He chuckles, his hands crossing over my back. "I'm starting to see that."

Dante's face appears younger when I look down at him this way. Free of stress lines, the corners of his mouth and eyes soft. I trace his lips with my finger. "I mean it. I rely on you for so much. Too much, really. But it's okay to let some of that go. I can be a partner. A *real* partner."

He sits up, bringing me with him so I'm straddling his hips and we meet face-to-face. My hair falls over my shoulders, the ends teasing along his chin. He brushes it back before taking my chin and meeting me for a kiss.

"I've never had a partner before, but I'm going to try, Frankie. I'm going to really, honestly try."

19

FRANKIE

"So. What should we do today?" I ask, digging into my black truffle and crab frittata.

Dante raises a brow at me from across the small table at the Grill.

I have to laugh. "*Aside* from sex."

"Hmm..." He looks off in thought as he chews a bite of smoked salmon benedict.

"We should probably spend at least a little time vertical," I add. "I picked the hotel, so you get to pick the activities."

He pauses before answering, a pensive look crossing his face. This is the most serious I've seen him since we got here. "I'm actually not sure. I've never really taken a vacation."

I set my fork down. "*Never* had a vacation?"

"Not really. My father said vacations were for people with nothing important to do."

"Oh, you poor little rich boy," I tease. One corner of

his mouth turns up when he catches my expression. "Mind if I take the reins on the activities, then?"

He leans back in his chair, his lips pulling into a line. "Okay..."

I can't help smiling. "Why do you sound so uncertain?"

"Because I can just imagine what's going on in that head of yours."

"Maybe you should be scared, then." I've been tossing an idea around, and his good-natured sarcasm just cemented it. I lean toward him with a look of concern. "One question. Do you even own a pair of hiking boots?"

"No," he says firmly.

"I figured as much," I say, shaking my head. "I'm gonna need to make a couple calls."

An hour later we're in Dante's car, our brand-new boots still wrapped up in their boxes in the back seat, along with a tote full of supplies I requested—it turns out having a personal butler included with your suite actually comes in handy. I only had to make one call.

Dante is driving, but he has no idea where we're going. I've been feeding him directions little by little along the way. We go up the 101 about twenty miles and then turn off at San Rafael, eventually making our way to a street lined with shops, restaurants, and cute cafés, the marquee of the Rafael theater visible just down the block.

He looks at me quizzically as I instruct him to pull over and park. "This is our activity?"

I laugh. "Not quite. Just sit tight. I'll be right back."

With that, I give him a quick kiss and run into my

159

favorite Puerto Rican restaurant to pick up the massive order I placed on my takeout app before we left the St. Regis. I give the huge to-go bag a little jiggle as I return to the car and arrange it securely in the back seat.

"What is in that extremely delicious smelling bag?" Dante asks as I buckle my seat belt.

"You'll find out soon enough, I promise. For now, just drive."

He shrugs as he checks traffic and pulls back onto the road. I direct him to head northeast and then turn onto Sir Francis Drake. We get about a mile before he shoots me another questioning look. "What's the next turn?"

I never realized how much this man hate surprises. "Don't worry, I know the way," I tell him with a smile. "I could practically get us there with my eyes closed."

As we continue on our drive, I probe him gently for more about his childhood. Not surprisingly, it was a lonely one—with a father who pitted brother against brother, and the Bellanti family as a whole against the world. I can tell Dante hasn't spoken about it much in the past, because he doesn't sound rehearsed or bored the way people do when they've had to tell the same stories over and over again. It's almost like he's processing things out loud as the words tumble out of his mouth in fits and starts.

In turn, I share more about my upbringing as well. Dante already knows that my mother left early on, but I tell him anecdotes about my dad using me and my sisters as props to either fool people into thinking he was a dedicated family man, or to get himself—a quote-unquote hardworking single father, doing his best to care for us all on his own—out of a scrape.

I talk about how determined I was to learn more about vinification in Tuscany, how I had all these plans to come back and help turn the Abbott Winery around. I really believed I was going to save the family business. I stop short of saying that I wasn't surprised to find out my dad had sold me off to be married instead. It would ruin an otherwise promising day.

Shifting gears, I tell another humorous story, this one about the time Dad left me and my sisters in London while he went off to Monte Carlo to gamble in some big tournament.

"I was twelve at the time, Charlie was sixteen. He left her in charge of Livvie and me but didn't leave us any money. The credit card he had on file got declined, so I had to sweet talk the hotel manager into letting us stay until he came back. Even though I had no idea if he would."

"So what did you do all day, wait around in the room? Or did you three just run amok around London?" Dante asks, a concerned edge in his voice. "I mean, you had to eat, right?"

I shrug. "Nothing too crazy. We mostly stayed in the room. Charlie convinced the pub down the road to let her work bussing tables, so she'd bag up all the leftover fish and chips and stale soda bread after her shift and bring it back to us with her tips. I just wish Dad had left us in France—at least the bar food would have been good, right?"

MY VOICE IS LIGHT, as if the whole thing was a great lark, but just thinking of it now brings back the fear and uncertainty we felt, not knowing if he'd abandoned us for good, or if he'd gotten into some kind of trouble and wouldn't even be able to come back. It suddenly clicks why Rico abandoning me in Roccette hit me so hard. Why I shut down so completely afterward.

Dante takes my hand and squeezes, letting me know that he understands.

I watch the scattered fall colors whisk by, the trees interspersed with more and more evergreens, fragrant conifers, and cedars. As the elevation increases, I roll the window down and breathe in the cool, fresh air. Soon, I'm directing Dante onto a winding, hilly road, one that will take us far away from anyone but ourselves and pure nature.

"Okay. Turn left. Almost there," I say, pointing at a narrow gravel road that leads into the dense trees. A little further along, I see the two circular red reflectors nailed into the trunk of a familiar western red cedar and say, "This is it. You can park."

"Here?" he asks, pulling onto the side of the road. "We're in the middle of nowhere."

"You trust me, right?" I ask with a wink.

Without waiting for an answer, I get out and grab our new boots from the back seat. Once we're properly shod, Dante grabs the food bag and my overstuffed tote bag and lets me lead him down a dirt path into the woods.

A few yards in, the dirt gives way to sand and opens up onto a small, secluded beach surrounded by scrubby trees. The lake is crystal blue, a mirror of the sky. Green hills, spotted with sprawling oaks and pines, roll into the horizon across the water. The air is brisk and the breeze is cool, but with the bright sun overhead, it's a perfect Nor Cal fall day.

"Welcome to Tomales Bay," I say grandly.

I lift my face to the sun and breathe in deep, but when I look back over at Dante, he's staring at me, not the scenery. His eyes are alight and awed, as if I'm somehow more beautiful than the view. It turns my heart right over.

I grab a blanket out of the tote and spread it out on the sand. Then I gesture for Dante to hand me the to-go bag and begin pulling out the boxes of food. Pasteles wrapped in banana leaves, tostones, bistec sandwiches on light, crispy bread, and coconut soda.

After a slight pause, Dante sinks down next to me, not exactly looking comfortable. He starts digging around in the bag like he's looking for something.

"They forgot utensils." He flips the bag over just in case they're hiding somewhere, clearly annoyed.

Smiling, I break the news to him: "Good, because you do *not* eat tostones with a fork. You have much to learn, young padawan."

Popping open the container, I grab a fried plantain and lift it to his mouth. He hesitates for a second and then takes a small bite.

"It's...good," he says, sounding surprised.

I shake my head and laugh, handing him one of the

sandwiches. As he starts unwrapping the paper from it, I pull a bottle of white wine out and open it.

"This is the absolute best wine pairing I've ever tasted," I tell him. "It's a fourteen-dollar bottle and it is going to blow your mind."

"Let me guess," he says dryly. "No glasses."

"Not a one," I agree, taking a sip from the bottle and letting the cool, crisp, rich flavor burst over my tongue.

I open my eyes and pass him the bottle. Dante drinks. He's impressed, but he only shows it with the raise of an eyebrow. High praise, indeed.

Feeling smug, I dig into my sandwich. We eat in silence for a few moments. Out of the corner of my eye, I spy Dante visibly relaxing, taking in the scenery, enjoying his meal. He even reaches for the wine bottle and takes several more drinks before handing it over to me.

"You seem different," he says, pulling the box of tostones closer. "More...I don't know. Just different."

"Yeah. I guess I finally realized something last night." I look out over the water. "My dad has nothing he can hold over me anymore. I should've gotten Livvie out of the house sooner, but losing the horses—as devastating as it is for her—I can't help thinking it saved us. It's like he cut away the one string that kept us tied to the compound."

A familiar pressure settles on my chest. The ever present feeling of not being enough, not doing enough. The guilt over not being there for Livvie during the last few years.

"Now that she's at Charlie's," I add, "Clayton and his connections should be powerful enough to protect Livvie, I think. And I mean, Charlie is practically her mother anyway. She should have moved in there years ago..."

"You did your best," Dante says soothingly. "You've all done your best."

I nod, mulling it over. "You seem a little different to me too, actually."

He swallows a bite of his steak sandwich and cocks his head. "Oh?"

"Just look at you. Sitting on the ground, eating with your hands. Drinking out of a bottle. You're practically a savage."

We both laugh, and Dante takes another swig of wine as if to prove my point.

"But no...it's good to see you looking a little less buttoned up. A little more...human."

"I'm not that bad," Dante insists.

"Are too," I say, reaching out to cup his cheek. "Always in control. Never a hair out of place, never a button undone—except to show how casually cool you can be."

"You think I'm cool?" he says.

"Don't get all full of yourself now."

He sets the last bit of his sandwich down, reaches up, and unbuttons his top button. As he holds my gaze, he moves his fingers to the next button. He slowly releases that one, and then another, and another.

"I like where this is going," I purr, leaning back to watch the impromptu strip show going on in front of me.

His shirt hits the ground, and I take in the delicious way his white undershirt clings to every muscle—of course he would wear an undershirt on a vacation day. He seems to know exactly what I'm thinking as he peels it up his torso and slips it over his head.

Standing, he leans down to pull off his new hiking boots. Next he grins cockily and unfastens his pants, letting them drop to the ground. My mouth falls open as he kicks them away and stands before me, buck-ass nude on the beach.

"Dante Bellanti, I do believe you are indecently exposed. And in public, no less."

He spreads his arms wide and makes a little turn, showing off for me. His smile is so big, his whole body seems to smile too.

Suddenly, he takes off toward the water. He runs in confident, long-legged strides, barely slowing until the water reaches his mid-thigh. Then he dives in, disappearing for a moment and popping up farther out than where he went in, shaking water out of his hair.

I stand and watch, laughing as he lets loose an exhilarated whoop.

"How cold is it?" I shout.

"Slightly more than anticipated!" he yells back, splashing around.

Did he just make an actual joke?

"Come in with me!" he demands.

Cackling, I cross my arms over my chest. "Not on your life! It must be freezing!"

I'm never one to turn away from a challenge, but I

draw the line at hypothermia. He disappears beneath the surface again and I kneel back down on the blanket to start packing up our picnic, stuffing all the boxes and napkins and foil into the to-go bag.

I'm just reaching for his discarded clothes when I hear the sound of crunching sand—just a fraction too late to react in time. Dante's cold, wet, very strong arms wrap around me from behind. His lips are warm as he kisses the back of my neck and works his way to my ear.

"Didn't you know that this is a nude beach?" he informs me.

"You better not," I say, but he's already unbuttoning the front of my sundress, sliding my denim jacket off at the same time.

In seconds, he strips me naked and lays me down on the sun-warmed blanket. I'm a little chilled by the breeze and the drops of lake water that fall off Dante onto my bare skin, but his body is hot as he pushes his cock into me, taking my face in his hands for a hungry kiss.

I don't have time to think about what we're doing or *where* we're doing it as he thrusts in perfect rhythm. Soon there's nothing but heat and skin and pleasure, and the sound of our moans.

This is making love. This is the thrill of the sky above, the earth below, and the man inside me, both grounding me and setting me free. He works me with his cock, taking his time with his strokes so I can feel every inch of him. I give it back in full measure, tensing the muscles at my core as I meet his every thrust.

"I love you," Dante says, over and over again.

"I love you, too," I tell him, emotion making my breath catch in my throat.

Our words pour out of us until we can no longer speak, only moan. I wrap my legs around his waist and cross my ankles, tilting my hips higher, helping him drive even further into me so we're locked together, the sweet tension inside drawing tighter and tighter.

"Frankie—"

And then he's coming inside me, groaning with every hot spurt, as hard and deep as I've ever felt him. I dig my fingers into his back and hold him tight as he finishes, wishing I could draw this moment out forever. He relaxes over me like warm clay afterward, sighing softly, his fingers trailing in my hair. We lay like that until the breeze begins to cool us again.

After a while, he stands up and pulls me up with him. Shaking off the blanket, he wraps us up in it, my back pressed against his chest, his arms around my waist. I drowsily lean back into him, feeling the rise and fall of his breath along with mine. When his hand steals down between my legs, I laugh.

"Again?"

He gently pushes into me, his finger curling back to hit the spot that always makes me shiver. "No," he says, his voice a low rumble in my ear. "This is just for you."

As I stand and watch the wind ripple across the lake, Dante works me with his clever fingers, drawing me to a sweet and all-encompassing release. And when my knees give out with the strength of my climax, he's there to keep me steady. He holds me tight the entire time.

20

FRANKIE

Dante looks perfectly disheveled as he sits behind the wheel. His messy hair strays in the breeze coming in through the open windows, and he's left the top buttons of his shirt undone. I like this relaxed version of him—I hope this isn't the last I'll see of it.

We're back on the gravel road again, driving through thick trees. The leaves on the black oaks are flaming orange, and the maples are turning gold. I love being here in the fall.

I tell Dante to take the next right, and the road narrows to a bumpy dirt lane marked only by well-worn tire tracks. A beautiful, secluded little A-frame materializes at the end of the trail.

"Here we are," I say, pointing to the cabin. The front is all big picture windows, the sharp slope of the roof giving the house a fairy-tale quality, and the porch wraps around so you get a great view of the bay. "Home sweet home."

I nearly jump out of the car before he's even put it into park. It's been so long since I've been here, and I'm overjoyed to be back. I grab my bag and nearly skip to the front door.

Dante comes up behind me and puts a hand on my shoulder. "Is this your family's place?"

"It belongs to the Alvarezes," I explain as I punch a code into the lock box—Delores's birthday—and then take out a set of keys. "I spent many hours of my childhood here with Delores and her family."

"It was kind of her to offer you the place for the weekend," he says.

"Yeah. She actually mentioned it last week, but I only thought to take her up on it now."

I unlock the front door and swing it wide. Dante carries the bags in first, and I flip on the lights and watch as he makes a slow rotation around the main room.

The A-frame is quaint but idyllic, with wall-to-wall wood paneling and lots of windows. Upstairs is a loft with a railing that lets you look down on the living room, and a wrought iron chandelier hangs from the peaked ceiling. The living area and kitchen are all one big room, with a stone fireplace along the wall creating a visual divider between the spaces. Two small bedrooms are tucked away behind the kitchen, along with the bathroom.

I trail my fingers over the furniture as I give Dante the tour. The familiar but dated mauve, beige, and hunter green color scheme brightens the living area with unapologetically 1980s grandma flare, along with

Delores's handmade crochet doilies and porcelain animal collection taking up every spare inch of space.

"Wow. How, um..." Dante gestures to a figurine on a side table—a cat with a bow around its neck.

"How adorable? Quirky? Cheesy?" I supply.

"Vintage," he finishes.

"Nice save," I say. "And yes, they're all hideous. But I love them. I love this whole place. It's exactly perfect."

"It's great. Better than the St. Regis."

I can't tell if he's joking or not. "Really?"

"Really," he says.

Warmth floods my chest at his appreciation. "I think so, too."

We choose the loft bedroom and set down our things. Then I take his hand and lead him out the back door and into the waiting woods.

Our afternoon is spent walking the highlands and taking in the views from the highest hills before the wind turns cold and finally chases us back inside.

Dante gathers an arm full of split logs from the wood box outside and sets about making a fire while I head to the kitchen to see what's available in the pantry. I pretend like I'm really focused on looking for food, but really I'm watching him from the corner of my eye to see if he knows what he's doing.

He methodically arranges a few of logs in the grate, then adds crumpled newspaper and twigs between them for kindling, and then sets a few more logs on top like a good Boy Scout. Minutes later, a small, crackling fire lights up the fireplace. He patiently watches the flames, making minor adjustments until a solid fire is burning.

I'm impressed. For a man who's never had a proper vacation, he managed that like a pro. I take down two cans of tomato soup and dump them into a pot on the stove. Then I open a box of mac and cheese and fill up a saucepan with water, setting it to boil. Dante walks over and looks curiously at the stove.

"Gourmet enough for you?" I tease.

"Looks great. Then again, I'm probably hungry enough to eat cardboard."

"Ha ha," I say, wrapping my arms around him. "Think you can handle the macaroni while I shower?"

Dante frowns, looking dubiously at the box on the counter.

"You *have* cooked before..." I sort-of ask.

He levels me with a stare that might mean anything, but I just laugh.

"Just follow the directions on the box. If anything catches on fire, throw it in the bay."

Turns out that Dante manages just fine. By the time I get out of the shower he's got two bowls of soup set on doily placemats on the table, along with plates of mac and cheese topped with parmesan and black pepper. He even lit the decorative taper candles in the center.

"Fancy," I say, grinning.

His eyes sweep over me as I saunter to the table in my satin sleep shorts and matching camisole. He pulls out the chair for me, his fingers caressing the side of my neck before he snaps open a fabric napkin and sets it on my lap.

"This is going to be the finest shelf-stable meal you've ever had. Chef's promise."

I grin at him across the table. "Considering I never checked the expiration date on the box, I'm going to let you taste it first. *Chef.*"

He takes his seat across from me and spears me with another heated look. "I'm much more excited about dessert."

I swallow hard, and suddenly food is the last thing on my mind. How can he always make me want him, just like that? One look, one perfectly dropped word. Every single time.

We're able to work our way through the meal, which is better than decent, but the second our spoons are down, Dante drags my chair away from the table and scoops me up in his arms.

"I'm taking you upstairs," he says, his voice low.

The possessive timbre of his voice sends lusty chills down my spine. "It would be a shame to waste this gorgeous fire. Maybe we should put the futon mattress—"

I don't have to tell him twice. After setting me down, Dante drags the mattress over to the fireplace and sets it on the floor. My heart thumps with anticipation as he holds out his hand to me. I take it, and he pulls me down beside him, guiding me back onto the cushions.

Closing my eyes, I let myself relax as he undresses me by the light of the fire. When I'm naked before him, his hard body covers mine, his lips finding the curve of my neck as he plants hot kisses there. My fingers slide into his silky hair as he trails kisses over my collarbone and along my shoulder, making me shiver.

His hands and lips are suddenly everywhere. He drops a kiss on my belly, his thumb sliding down to stroke the wetness between my legs. Opening for him, I guide his head lower until his mouth is so close I can feel his warm breath on my pussy. Without warning his tongue plunges inside me, making me gasp. I spread myself wider for him, giving him better access, my other hand firm on the back of his head as he feasts on me.

Heat from the fire warms my skin. It joins the heat only Dante can flame in me until I'm burning with need. The fire crackles in time with my breathless panting as he tongue-fucks me, bringing me closer...closer.

I clasp both of my hands behind his head and hold him firm as I take control, riding his mouth, throwing my head back. Knowing there's nobody around for miles, I let loose, moaning as loud as I can. The sounds of my pleasure, echoing off the cabin walls, push me to an even higher level. I'm so wet, so ready to come, grinding against Dante's face faster and faster.

The fire suddenly bursts in an array of sparks as my climax barrels over me. Gasping through the shockwaves of the orgasm, I can't help but laugh at the sight of sparks raining down in the fireplace.

"Fireworks for the big finale," Dante whisper-laughs as he sits back on his knees.

I can see the bulge in his jeans, and even though I'm nearly limp with pleasure, I'm not going to leave that fat cock untasted. Crawling over to him, I unbutton his jeans and work the zipper down. Once his pants are down far enough for his dick to spring free, I push him onto his back and take him in my mouth.

He groans, his fingers weaving into my hair as I begin feasting on him like he did to me. He swells immediately, his hips jerking to the movement of my hot, sucking mouth. I can taste his salty precum, and he's already so hard that I know he won't last long.

"Frankie—"

He tries to pull back, but I grip his hips and hold him in place, drinking him down as he explodes in the back of my throat.

"Mmm," I moan, my mouth full of him.

"*Fuck.*" He presses himself hard down my throat one last time and then withdraws, his heated eyes on me while I lick my lips and fall back against the mattress.

I watch as he stands and kicks his jeans all the way off, then crouches to rummage through the pockets. "What're you doing?" I ask.

My eyes are heavy, exhaustion hitting me like a brick.

"Go to sleep," he says gently.

"I sleep better with you next to me."

Dante grabs a blanket off the back of the cushionless futon and spreads it over me, then crawls underneath and pulls me close.

"Look at that," I say, pointing up at the windows full of stars above us.

We lay there, linked together, sighing contentedly at the sight of a million pinpoints of light dotting the midnight sky through the glass. I watch the stars until I can't keep my eyes open any longer and wake to the sun streaming down where our personal galaxy had been.

Later that morning, we're back on the road. This time, he doesn't question my directions.

"Someone's finally relaxing enough to give up some control," I tease, ruffling his hair.

"That's because someone else once told me that good things happen when I trust you," he says. "And she hasn't been wrong yet."

Grinning at his humor, I point to a road sign ahead. "Take the next left."

Soon, we've reached the tiny town of Two Rock. I double-check the directions on my phone and instruct Dante to turn onto a long driveway that leads to a farm populated by several sprawling greenhouses.

"What is this place?" he asks.

"Research," I admit. "I've been wanting to propose some changes to the vineyard, so I actually started emailing with Raya, the owner, last month. She propagates herbs here. She said she'd be happy to meet with me and show me the farm, and since we were in the area..."

"I thought we were on vacation," Dante says, his voice teasing.

"We are. But all play and no work makes...something-something."

He laughs at my lame joke attempt, and I'm glad to know I haven't burst our vacation bubble by bringing him here. Once we park, I spot a middle-aged woman in a pair of classic denim overalls, a long braid, and a flannel shirt approaching our car.

"Raya?" I ask, getting out and waving. "It's Frankie, from Bellanti Vineyards."

"Frankie!" she says with a smile. "Welcome. And who is this strapping young lad?"

Dante comes around the car and I introduce him as the owner of the vineyard. As Raya gives us a full walking tour of the farm's growing operations, I explain to her and Dante about companion crops.

"We're already growing mustard on the property to attract pollinators, just like everyone else in Napa," Dante says.

"Exactly! Everyone *else* does it," I say. "Which is why we should switch to hyssop."

I throw out my arm, gesturing at the long, parallel rows of soft purple flowers that make up Raya's hyssop field. The herb gives off a sweet, almost medicinal smell, but the bees love it.

"It's a cash crop," Raya chimes in. "Always in high demand."

"You know what else?" I add, thinking out loud. "All those purple flowers would be a great destination for the Instagram tourists, too. And what about clover?"

"Attracts more bees than mustard," Raya says with a nod. "And you can cut it and sell it for hay. I harvest my red clover twice in the summer and once in late fall. Only takes about half a week to dry and bale."

"We *have* to rotate the crop," I urge Dante, my voice

pitching higher with excitement. "If we do, it'll help rejuvenate the soil. Our vines will be *thriving*."

Back at the car, I notice Raya has a huge smile on her face. She probably doesn't get many random visitors, not to mention ones as enthusiastic about her farming techniques as I am.

"Crop rotation really works," she says. "I do the same thing with my sprouting fields."

Dante looks skeptical. "How are all these new crops going to affect the grapes, though?"

"That's what Abbott can be. Or part of it, at least. A testing ground. Give my plan five years, and I *guarantee* the Abbott vines will be outproducing yours of the same variety."

My smile drops as I remember that there's still a major complication to address.

"This is assuming we pay off Rico for his half-ownership of the Abbott compound," I add. "I'm positive he'd prefer cash over having to actually battle for his rights to the property in court. He was bluffing when he said he wanted to try to get the winery up and running again."

Dante's expression turns steely. "Let's not worry about that fly in the ointment just yet." Turning to Raya, he spreads his hands. "What'll we need for two acres of each crop?"

After arranging deliveries for next spring, we get back in the car and hit the road. I'm sad to leave our vacation behind, but it's getting late so I tell Dante we can go home.

When we get back to Napa, Dante surprises me by

pulling into my father's place and driving out to the rolling vineyards. Then he has me show him where all the different fields would go. I'm happy to lay it out for him, taking into account the wind, water drainage, and sun angles in relation to planting our test crops. After I'm done, he gives me a slow nod.

"I think this just might work."

I'm almost afraid to ask, but I give voice to my biggest fear. "What about Rico?"

"I'll take care of it," Dante says. "Trust me. Everything is going to be okay."

Somehow, I believe him. "I do trust you."

Smiling, he picks me up and swings me around in a circle, pulling me into a long kiss.

Then he sets me down and digs something out of his pocket. He holds it out to me. Looking closer, I realize he's holding a ring—a beautiful old cut diamond with Art Deco swirls of platinum and emeralds around it. I go completely still, my heart caught in my throat.

"It belonged to my grandmother, and I'd like you to have it," he says. "But it comes with one condition." He cups my face between his hands. "You'd have to marry me again."

I give a little shake of my head. I can't believe this is happening. "It can't just be about the land," I say. "It includes Charlie and Livvie, too."

He smiles. "I know the Abbott sisters are a package deal. And I'd be honored to have them as part of our family. Charlie is the best event planner we've ever hired, so she'll have a job with Bellanti Vineyards as long as she wants one."

"And Livvie, too," I whisper, my voice choked up with emotion.

"Armani already located and purchased two of her horses so far. They're being boarded in a stable across town."

"Dante." My jaw drops. I know for a fact that the purebred Friesians could only have been bought back at great cost to the Bellantis.

"Anything is worth having you in my life. That's what family is. I forgot that somewhere along the way, or maybe my father tried to beat it out of me, but if you want to be with me, we can take care of each other until the end of time. It's your choice."

I can't help the tears streaming down my face. He's offering me a choice. The chance to decide my own fate, once and for all. But there's only one choice to make.

It feels like a dream as I wrap my arms around him, drawing his face close to mine for a kiss. "I'll marry you again. Hell, three times if it'll do the trick."

Laughing, he slides the ring onto my finger. "Why not make it four?"

He looks so handsome when he laughs, I'm determined to make sure he does it more often. At least once a day. For the rest of our lives.

21

FRANKIE

I WAKE UP SLOWLY, contentedness wrapped as tight around me as Dante's arms are. Stretching, I catch a glimpse of something flashing in the morning light.

It's the ring on my left hand, reminding me that I'm going to marry the right man this time. For real. We'd ended our little honeymoon last night with dinner on Dante's balcony, followed by another round of lovemaking.

I keep waiting for it to become routine or less powerful, but every time we come together, it feels richer. Deeper. Like our connection just keeps getting stronger.

He's slow to wake up as I rub his back. I debate starting something lovely with him again, but when I glance at the clock I realize it's late—almost eight a.m. It's time to begin my day.

"I'm going for a run," I whisper, giving Dante one last kiss before I roll out of bed and head to the bathroom to change into workout clothes.

"Be safe," he calls after me. "Don't forget your phone."

Outside, the sun is bright and brilliant as I jog down the road. I'd love to just bask in the afterglow of our little vacation, but unfortunately, the real world is waiting. I have things to take care of. Things to clear out of the way so Dante and I can get on with our lives.

Without breaking my stride, I pull out my cell and call Rico. A queasy feeling goes through me just seeing his name on my screen, but I need to get this over with. Because even though Dante promised to take care of the Rico situation, it's my mistake. My responsibility.

Plus, I might be able to reason with him. Negotiate a deal that we can both live with. The Bellantis can pay some agreed-upon sum for Rico's half of the Abbott Winery, and in exchange Rico can sign divorce papers and disappear.

That's the best outcome I've been able to dream up, anyway.

The phone rings and rings and finally goes to voice-mail. "Dammit," I curse to myself.

I'm both frustrated and relieved as I tap out a text.

Hi, Rico. We need to speak—and soon.

It takes another mile and a half for me to clear my head and return to the house. I find Dante in the shower when I get upstairs, cleaning up after his own morning workout routine. I quickly strip out of my leggings and sports bra and join him under the steamy water.

He reaches for me, obviously pleased that I've chosen to join him.

"How was your run?"

I run my hands down his strong arms. "Not enough to wear me out."

"Don't tempt me." He grins. "We're already running late and we need to head down for breakfast. But I will take a raincheck."

We content ourselves with light kisses, and then quickly towel off and get dressed. As we hold hands and make our way downstairs, I can't help thinking that we have a whole lifetime of togetherness ahead of us. And that for once, I feel the certainty of a man's love.

In the dining room, Armani and Marco don't bat an eye when they see me slide into the chair beside Dante's. Actually, Marco does bat an eye—in a saucy wink—but then he passes me the coffee pot, and I feel like I've been accepted into the family again.

It's almost as if I never left.

"Good morning," I say cheerily.

Armani glances up from his tablet screen as I pour myself a coffee. "Glad you're here, Frankie. I've tracked down some more of your family's horses."

"That's amazing!" I gush. "I can't thank you enough for doing this."

Alain appears with plates of food, including my favorite Tuscan style omelet, made extra cheesy, with rustic toast and fruit on the side. I'm touched that he prepared it my first day back, and I mouth a "thank you" to the chef as he sets my plate before me.

"I've managed to locate four of the Friesians so far," Armani continues, "but I'm afraid the rest of them have been sold across the country already. They'll be harder for me to track."

I nod, chewing my toast slowly. It takes several heart-beats before I work up the nerve to ask, "Which ones were you able to find?"

He consults his tablet. "Let me see...we have Maelje, Ytse, Maximum...and Avina." He taps around on the screen some more. "I may have another lead, or at least I think so, but—"

He doesn't get a chance to finish as I all but race around the table to wrap him in a hug. Armani seems shocked, his entire body going tense, and I feel him turn his head to look across the table at his brother. The fact that Dante is smiling at us, looking pleased, is probably even more shocking to Armani than my unexpected PDA.

I pull away and pat Armani on the shoulder, composing myself as best I can after my outburst of appreciation. "Thank you. So much. You have no idea what this means to us."

A whisper of a smile crosses his lips. "You're welcome."

I take my seat again and pick up my fork, but I know I won't be able to eat anything. I can't wait to tell Livvie the good news. Dante reaches under the table and takes my hand.

"There's more," he says.

"More?" I echo. "Are you serious?"

Marco digs into his bacon and eggs while watching us, as if he also can't wait to hear the news. Dante takes a slow sip of his coffee, drawing out my anticipation just for fun.

"I'm going to have a gate installed in the property fence that separates the Abbott vines from the Bellanti vines. This way the Friesians will be safe at the stables where we keep our trail riding horses for the guests, but Livvie could easily ride over to the Abbott property to use the arenas and keep up with her training. Oh—and do you think Livvie might want to move into the guesthouse? It would make her commute to school a lot quicker and less stressful—"

This time it's Dante who gets my arms thrown around him.

After breakfast, I check my phone again. Of course, there's nothing from Rico. I leave him a curt voicemail and send another text to say we really need to talk, so we can "resolve the situation to our mutual benefit." I use those specific words on purpose—Rico-speak for somebody getting paid off. I figure the implication of money exchanging hands will get him to return my call faster.

On a whim, I scroll through my contacts and try my dad's cell number, but it goes to voicemail without even ringing. Probably shut off for nonpayment, or maybe he turned it off to hide from everyone, including his own daughters. What a piece of shit. How he ever managed to have three kids with the same woman, I'll never know. He didn't deserve us. Any of us.

I look down at my ring and can't help wondering what kind of mother would have seen the kind of man my father is and then left her children with him anyway. It's a question I've struggled with ever since Mom walked out on us. Because although I don't blame her for leaving him, I can't forgive her for not taking us, too.

And I swear to God, if I ever have children of my own, I'll never do the same.

22

FRANKIE

IT FELT amazing to walk into work at the Bellanti offices today, to sit down in my fancy ergonomic Aeron chair behind my gleaming new desk, in an office right down the hall from Dante. I've got a hot coffee in my hand, my laptop open, and I'm raring to go.

The staff seem happy to see me, if a bit wary and unsure about the office politics—especially with Jessica being let go for the second time in a row—but I'm determined to put any and all drama behind us.

Mid-morning, I ask Ruby, the main receptionist and office administrator, to come in and see me so I can chat with her and get a better sense of how the vineyard's record keeping and financial planning works. Soon enough she's showing me the books, huge binders full of printouts from our management software, complete with detailed budget breakdowns.

"This is great," I tell her. "I can't believe you have to keep on top of so much stuff."

"You have no idea. Glad to know someone appreciates it," she says.

"I'm going to get you a raise," I promise. "And an assistant. And a cake."

She laughs. "Two out of three, and I'll never retire."

After expressing my gratitude again, I send her away and dive right in. Before I know it, I've spent an hour catching up on all the Bellanti Vineyard's books, including the itinerary and budget for the upcoming End of Harvest Gala that Charlie organized. I've been excited for this event since its conception, and as the days grow shorter, and the fall colors richer, my excitement grows. I have so much to do.

There's a knock on my door shortly after lunch. Marco pops his dark head in and gives a sheepish grin. I was expecting him hours ago.

"I'm here to give you a tour around the fields." He steps fully into my office and I'm slightly surprised to see him dressed casually.

"You mean the tour that was supposed to happen at nine a.m.?" I ask, lifting a brow.

He gives me a grin that I'm sure he uses to get exactly what he wants—and I have no doubt that it works. "I had a fast weekend with my car at the races. Thought I deserved a slow morning to recuperate."

I roll my eyes good-naturedly and stand from behind my desk. He gives me a once-over.

"You might want to change your clothes. A pencil skirt isn't going to cut it."

"I'm not sure if I'm more curious about what you

have planned, or impressed that you know what a pencil skirt is."

He winks. "I only know skirts by how quickly they can be removed. Those have zippers straight down the back. One pull and they're off." He pauses. "I suppose talking this way is against office policy. But you're family, so does it really count?"

"It counts. I'll let it slide this one time." I wave him out of my office. "Let's go."

On our way out, we hear Armani and Candi chatting in his office. Her voice is light and friendly, while his is even more stilted and quiet than usual. Marco gives me a knowing glance, and I grin. Whatever is going on between those two, Armani can't fight it forever.

I pop into the main house to change into jeans. When I get back outside I see Marco waiting in the yard, holding the reins of a horse in each hand.

"Ytse!" I shout. I all but float over to the gelding.

Marco hands me the reins with a smile. He chose a large buckskin for himself. I'm so happy to get back on my horse that I can barely stand it.

I let Marco give me a boost into the saddle and then lean forward to wrap my arms around Ytse's neck. He gives a toss as if welcoming me and paws a hoof in the dirt. Marco mounts up and leads the way. As I move up beside him, his gaze drops to my hand.

"Couldn't help noticing that ring on your finger. Might that be a Bellanti family heirloom?"

"Why, yes it is."

"Thank God," he says. "With you around, Dante

might actually become a Real Boy again. I never in a million years thought my brother would fall in love."

I laugh. "What about you, Marco?"

He puts a hand on his chest. "Me? I'm always in love. I fall in love every day. I'm never lonely!"

But despite his words, I hear a whisper of bitterness underneath the bravado. Such a dichotomy to his words. Knowing what I do of Dante's upbringing, I suspect that all three brothers are lonely in their own respects. They have each other, but they're not bonded the way my sisters and I are. The Bellantis' relationships strike me as more professional than intimate.

Nudging my horse closer, I ask, "What was it like, growing up with Dante?"

"You don't want to know." He laughs. "But seriously, he wasn't all that different. When he was younger, he was more full of anger I suppose. And much quicker to beat my ass."

I catch the same mix of sadness and bravado in his voice.

"Why do you think he was so angry?"

Marco's smile fades. "Come on, Frankie. I think you know the answer to that."

He makes a clicking sound to signal his horse to canter, and they take off over the first set of gentle hills. I nudge Ytse forward so we can catch up, and I'm out of breath when we finally come to a stop beside Marco. He's taking in the view of the vineyard's neat rows, the vines bursting with autumnal shades of russet and gold and deep, fiery red.

"Beautiful," I comment.

Marco nods. I expect him to take off again, but instead he starts to talk.

"Our father was a harsh man, but he was harshest on Dante," he says haltingly. "I was the troublemaker and probably punished the most, out of the three of us. But I didn't take anything to heart. The shit that Dad pulled just rolled off my back.

"But Dante isn't like me. He felt every mistake deep in his bones, and he never made the same misstep twice. Which made him careful, but also...miserable. And very cold. But then..."

There's a beat of silence. I'm holding my breath because I want him to continue.

"Then?" I ask gently.

"Then I saw the way he smiled at you at breakfast. He must really love you after all."

I'm not sure how to respond, but Marco and his buckskin take off again, so I don't have to. We don't stop until we reach the highest hill, where the horses finally get a chance to rest.

From our vantage point, he shows me the lay of the land, explaining the layout of the entire Bellanti property. He goes into the history of each section of the vineyard, which lines were planted when, where the starter vines came from, and how each section produces. I never pegged him as being overly involved in the family business, but the more he talks, the more I realize how invested he is. And how he might just be the cleverest of the Bellanti brothers. He's sharper than I ever gave him credit for.

Back at the vineyard stables, I spy Charlie's car coming up the drive. It's mid-afternoon, so she must be dropping off Livvie. Patting Ytse on the neck, I say, "Let's give them a little surprise, huh boy?"

I heel him into a gallop and fly down the vine rows. The horse easily hops the ditch and comes to a sliding stop right alongside the gravel drive. Charlie barely rolls to a stop before Livvie jumps out and races toward me. I dismount just in time to catch my sister in a big hug. Ytse tosses his head, but he's too cool to care about a bunch of squealing women.

Tears well up in Livvie's eyes. "How did this happen? Where did you find them?"

"Not all of them," I tell her gently. "Armani's been working on it. But we have the pregnant mares, Maeije and Avina. And Max."

Livvie can't hold back anymore. She bursts into sobs, burying her face in Ytse's mane. I rub her back in slow circles and Charlie comes over and wraps us all in a group hug. Marco clears his throat softly from behind us. I'd forgotten he was following Ytse and me.

"I'll take Ytse back to the stable so you all can be together," he offers.

Livvie whips him a look over her shoulder while wiping her eyes with one hand. "Not on your life! I'm gonna go see Max. Make sure he still remembers me."

She vaults into the saddle and nudges the big black horse toward the stables. Charlie and I watch as Livvie and Ytse take off, Marco giving chase, Livvie's laugh floating back to us.

"It's good to see her like this again," Charlie says.

I nod. "Is Clayton back yet?"

My sister's face falls and she shakes her head no. He's been away a long time.

"It's settled then," I tell her. "You're staying for dinner."

Before she can argue, I whip out my phone and text Alain to set out an extra plate. Then we get in the car and drive back to the main house. She asks about Dante and our weekend away, and I fill her in on some of the G-rated details.

"You know, he really seems to be trying. He's actually opening up to me."

Charlie doesn't look convinced. "I hope you're right. But I'll believe it when I see it."

"That's fair," I concede. Especially since she's my big sister—no man has ever been good enough for me in Charlie's eyes. "Do you want to come up to the main house, or can I set you up with some wine? I need to take a quick shower before dinner."

"How is that even a question? Wine is always the answer."

We park in the guest lot and I lead her into the tasting room. Armani and Candi are at a table by the big picture windows, apparently still engrossed in conversation. Candi waves in welcome and Charlie heads over to join them.

I motion for a server to send around the house red

before heading back to the main house. When I step out of the bathroom wrapped in one of Dante's robes, I find him in the bedroom changing. He's mostly undressed, and I take advantage of his bare torso, running my hands and lips all over him. As we start to kiss, quickly going from soft and sweet to hot and heavy, he slides his hands under the robe and palms my ass. I let out a soft moan.

"Dante," I pant.

"I'd love to keep going with this," he says between kisses, "but dinner."

"Fine." I pull back from him with a melodramatic sigh. "I suppose eating food is a thing."

We both finish dressing, but I can't help noticing that Dante looks like he has something on his mind. And even though we don't have time to get into it right now, I know we have things we need to discuss. Like Rico, for one.

"What's on your mind?" I ask, turning so he can zip up my light blue dress.

"I was just wondering if you'd heard from your father lately."

I turn back around and shrug. "He hasn't been in contact. Not that that's unusual for him, but...it's kind of been a while. What about the name I gave you? Any leads on Bregman?"

He frowns. "Armani's still working on it. No sign of him, as yet. It's like the guy dropped off the face of the planet without a trace. Which in itself is a red flag."

I wrap my arms around him, sharing in the mutual frustration for a moment before pulling away and taking his hand.

We enter the dining room to find the table pleasantly full. Charlie is there sipping a glass of wine, and Livvie and Marco sit side by side, smelling faintly of horse, but having one hell of a conversation considering the way she's slapping him with her napkin while he tries to grab it from her. Before I knew Marco better, I might have worried at his teasing. But it's clear he's not serious, and I know Livvie's not interested in him that way.

Smiling, I take my seat at the foot of the table, Dante at the head, Armani and Charlie to my left. The Livvie-Marco banter continues, and I tune in just in time to hear Livvie say, "Surprising, considering you're a total man ho," skewering Marco with a particularly well-placed barb.

I press my lips together, trying to suppress my laugh, but Marco takes it all in stride.

"Man ho I may be, but at least I go for what I want—unlike Armani, who collects interest but never cashes in."

Marco wags his eyebrows at his brother.

Armani coolly folds his hands on the table in front of them. "That may be true, but at least my penis won't fall off from some exotic STD."

Livvie snorts a laugh, and Dante takes the opportunity to cut in.

"Armani," he says reprovingly, "don't say 'penis.' There are ladies present."

Armani has the grace to look chastised. Marco sighs in annoyance at Dante's scolding.

"Say 'dick' instead," Dante continues. "I believe that's what the kids call it these days."

There's a collective intake. Did Dante just make a fucking *joke*? A stunned silence fills the room, and then the whole table erupts in laughter. Even Dante allows himself a self-satisfied smile and gives me a wink.

Marco slaps a hand on the table as he laughs. "If this is what having a wife does for Dante, we should have married him off years ago!"

23

FRANKIE

"Did I tell you about the time my daughter brought home a pet duck and thought she could keep it hidden from me in the shed? For weeks I'd let the poor thing out when she went to school, and he would follow me around the garden all day. She only realized I knew her little secret when she got off the bus one day and couldn't find him. She had a *complete* meltdown. We spent hours searching, until I was sure he had to've been scooped up by a hawk we had on the property, but then just before it got dark, we finally found him—he was napping under the azaleas!"

Raucous laughter sounds from the lively table of grandma-age Southern women I'm hosting in the tasting room. They've been telling stories about when their children were little for over an hour, interspersing each bout of laughter with more wine. I'm enjoying their company far more than I should be, considering I'm on the clock.

I rise from my seat and start to excuse myself, but

they insist that I stay and listen to just one more story. Since they're technically the only group I'm scheduled to host today, I'm happy to oblige. The tasting room is full in general, giving the staff more than enough to do. It's nice to hear so much laughter and conversation going on inside this building. Not to mention the obvious bonus of the profits we're making while everyone has a good time.

The oldest of the women, Arlene, leans forward to chime in with her deep, melodic Georgia accent. "Let me tell you about the time Harper and Alden tried to build a boat out of old milk jugs and some scrap lumber they found stacked up behind the barn."

"Oh no," one of the others says. "I bet I know where this is going."

"They worked on that thing for days, running in and out of the house asking for nails and rope and what have you. Problem was, none of the jugs had caps," Arlene says, shaking her head. "I didn't have the heart to tell 'em it wasn't gonna work, but they figured it out soon as they launched into the pond and tried to scramble on.

"Them jugs filled right up with water and they sank clear to the bottom. Maiden voyage didn't last much more than a few seconds, if that. Alden came home crying and missing a shoe, and I had to pretend I hadn't been watching 'em through the window the whole time!"

I laugh along with them and swap out their wine glasses for a new vintage. Their stories give me a warm, homey feeling, even though my home life was a far cry from what they're describing. I wonder what it would've been like to have a mom who'd been more like these women. Resilient, loving, good-humored. Just...there.

So far, I've heard about the baby blankets they knit for the neonatal ICU at the hospital, and how to make the best pie crust (you need to freeze the butter an hour beforehand, though a heated debate breaks out regarding whether shortening is superior). It's not all domestic talk, though—Arlene is a retired flight mechanic, and Elizabeth spent years traveling abroad as an antiques buyer.

I also learn about their town's biggest scandal this past year, which apparently involved their favorite hairdresser's illicit relationship with a dancer from the gentlemen's club. It has a happy ending, though—no pun intended—because after he put a ring on her finger, he paid for her to go to cosmetology school for her aesthetician's license. Now they co-own a salon together.

It's almost like I've stepped inside the world of a Hallmark movie. Everything about these women is wholesome, friendly, and family oriented. Well. Except for how shit-faced they're getting.

"Oooh, Mabel. Better fix your hat. That sweet thing at the bar is looking your way!"

The women giggle, one of them lowering her voice to say, "Now that is one tight ass."

Arlene leans toward Mabel. "Maybe you should go say hello, May. It's not every day you get a handsome man checking you out from across the room!"

Mabel shrugs. "He's probably just as drunk as the rest of us. I'll bet he doesn't know what he's looking at!"

I laugh along with them, enjoying their antics, but

when Elizabeth says he's getting up off the barstool, I sneak a peek his way. My heart skips a beat. It's Rico. He's leaning oh so casually against the bar, staring directly at me. *Shit.*

Why the hell did he just show up here? He never responded to a single message I left.

Mabel nudges me with her elbow, mistaking my shock for the good kind. "You should go over there. Introduce yourself. I see the ring on your finger, but you aren't married yet."

Oh, the irony. I'm being encouraged to hit on my legal husband, who I'm hoping to divorce, while wearing an engagement ring from my former, not-quite-legal husband, who I'm hoping to actually marry. Recovering, I clear my throat and compose myself.

"You know what, Mabel? I might just do that."

I crook a finger at Greg, the manager, in the universal "come here" gesture.

One of the ladies pats my arm. "Go get 'em, tiger. We'll be waiting for you."

"Oh, trust me, you'll like Greg better," I say. "He's got a very, very tight backside."

He comes over and I turn the ladies over into his care. They immediately begin to gush over his handsome dimples and ask him to turn around so they can get a better look at the goods.

I pass one of the servers on my way to the bar. "Go get Dante. *Now.*"

She nods and quickly rushes off, while I take my time walking to Rico. I don't want him to see how much he's unnerved me by being here. I'm also stalling for time, praying that Dante is still in his office right now.

Rico watches me approach with a smug expression. He makes an appreciative clicking sound with his tongue. "Well, well. Look at my sweet Francesca, all professional and fancy."

I don't take the bait. I gesture with my arm to the door, hoping I can herd him out of the tasting room. "Let's talk outside."

He smiles. "Afraid I'm going to make a scene?"

"We need to speak privately," I state flatly. "And it's too loud. We'll barely be able to hear each other talk."

"The only sound I need to hear is your pen writing several zeros on the check you're going to make out to me." Rico firmly plants himself against the bar, looking smug as shit.

My temples begin to throb. "Please don't make this difficult. I'm not going to discuss business with you in here."

Rico opens his mouth but then straightens suddenly, his face falling. I smell Dante's cologne before I see him, and then I feel the warm reassurance of his hand on my lower back, instantly steadying my shot nerves.

"Is there a problem here?" Dante asks, all menace.

Rico's eyes bounce from the ring on my hand to Dante's face and then back to me. "You two are looking cozy. So, I am happy to get out of your hair. Just pay me for my half of the Abbott vineyard. Simple." With that, he spreads his hands, the shit-eating grin back on his face.

"And do not think you are going to stiff me. I expect above market value."

"*What?*" I blurt, furious at his impudence.

He takes a slim manila envelope out of his blazer pocket and slaps it into my hand. "I had divorce papers drawn up. I will sign them as soon as I get my check."

Dante gently takes the envelope from me. But Rico's not done. He pulls out another piece of paper and opens the trifold. It's a bill of sale for the Abbott property.

My face flames hot. The muscles in the side of my neck tense and I feel an avalanche of rage crashing down inside me. I'm about to tell him to shove the papers up his profiteering, extortionary ass when Dante reaches for the bill of sale, too.

"I'll have my lawyers look over the documents and get back to you soon."

Rico smirks. "You have forty-eight hours."

Dante coolly tucks the paperwork into the inner pocket of his jacket. "You gain nothing by pressuring me. I'll make a determination when I'm ready."

Rico doesn't respond, just stares hard at us.

"By the way," Dante adds, leaning close enough to dominate Rico's personal space, "the next time Frankie calls, you'll pick up. Because the next time you set foot on my property, you will be escorted out by my very close and personal associates. And they will not be gentle."

Trying to look nonchalant about Dante's threat, Rico gives us a carefree salute and saunters toward the exit. On the way, he tosses a wink at my table of old ladies, making them all laugh like they're forty years younger.

Once he's out the door, they go back to their wine, tittering at being caught ogling Rico.

Meanwhile, all I feel is bile burning in the back of my throat.

Dante puts a hand on my arm. "I'm going to send a few guys to keep an eye on him as long as he's in town. Don't let him get to you."

"Easy for you to say."

I don't know why I'm so angry right now. Rico is just being Rico. But I'm fucking fuming. This isn't just about me or the money or the Abbott property itself. It's about this asshole making threats that affect the happiness and well-being of my whole family, compromising our legacy and our future without a second thought about anybody but himself.

Dante places a light kiss on my forehead, but I duck away before he can linger.

"Please tell Greg to take care of the rest of the tasting. I need some air." I step back.

"Frankie."

"I'll be here on time for the next one," I tell him.

With that, I make a beeline for the back door. Dante's voice is filled with concern as he calls out to me, but I don't stop or look over my shoulder. If I don't get away from my thoughts for a little while, I'll explode.

I don't know who I'm angrier at right now—Rico, or myself.

24

DANTE

"Pay him whatever he wants. Just get rid of him."

Back in my office, Armani has spent the last twenty minutes looking over the contract Rico gave Frankie. So far, my brother has said absolutely nothing to me about the validity of the terms, and I'm tired of pacing and waiting for him to speak up. I'll pay any price to get rid of this asshole and clear the path for Frankie and me.

Yet even though I'm more than ready to whip out my checkbook, I can't help but think that this whole thing is too easy. There has to be a catch. A man like Rico always wants more.

Armani finally looks up from the paperwork. "It looks legit to me. We can have the legal team review it in the morning."

"Have them look at it first thing. I want this done. I'm sick of wasting time on this prick."

I haven't seen Frankie since she left to take a breather. I'm concerned about her frame of mind—I'm sure she feels like she's made a terrible mess for herself—but I'm making an effort to respect her request for space. Hell, I know this whole thing has been a nightmare for her. She couldn't have possibly known what she was getting into when she married Rico.

Just like I had no idea what I was getting into when I agreed to marry her. I thought I was making a profitable business deal, and I was—but I got so much more.

Armani gathers the papers and taps them into order on the surface of his desk. "Well look at that, Dante. You're smiling again."

"I love her. And she loves me back. It's worth smiling about."

He dips his head. "I would advise you to hold off on signing anything just yet, even if our lawyers advise you to do so. I finally got a voicemail from someone at the Registrar of Vital Statistics in the city where Frankie got married, but with the nine-hour time difference, I haven't been able to get hold of someone during business hours so they can actually answer my questions. I think it would be wise to wait and hear what they have to say."

"Why would it matter?" My gut clenches. "Unless... does an Italian court have to handle the divorce proceedings for it to be legal? That could take months. Years, even."

"No." Armani shakes his head. "Frankie's domiciled here in the US, so she can get a legal divorce here in the states even if her marriage took place abroad. That's not an issue."

Relief washes over me. "Thank God. So then—"

Just then there's a knock at the door. Ruby, our admin, sheepishly pops her head in.

"Excuse me, Mr. Bellanti. And Mr. Bellanti. Um, Dante, Greg just called. It's almost time for the next wine tasting, but Frankie hasn't returned yet and she isn't answering her cell. Would you like him to cover her? He says it's no trouble."

Dammit. She must be more affected by Rico's little show this morning than I thought.

"Tell him to get everything prepped and to stand by, please," I say. "I'll go look for her."

"Very good."

She hurries away and I turn back to my brother. "Let me know the minute you hear from your Italian contact."

"Will do."

I leave the office and head to the tasting room to look for Frankie. I don't expect her to be there, but I take a cursory look around the kitchen, the stock room, and the retail area by the registers just in case she's wandering. Nothing. Knowing her, she's probably pacing the grounds and has completely lost track of time.

After circling the front of house one more time, I'm just about to exit the building when she walks in. My heart skips a beat when I see her. She looks collected and put together. Strong and poised. It hits me then just how lucky I am to have her.

"Frankie—" I reach for her, intending to give her a kiss on the cheek, but she sidesteps me and turns to engage with a customer.

Her brush-off stuns me for a moment, but then I

realize that she's probably wearing a very fragile mask right now—and that she's trying to keep all her walls up so she doesn't break down. No wonder she'd rather chat up a stranger than face me. She knows I'd be able to see through her brave façade better than anyone, and it might just push her over the edge.

Which I know because I'm basically the same way.

Giving her the space that I myself would want if our roles were reversed, I head back to my office. I keep tabs on her for the rest of the day, covertly. Once the tasting room closes for the day, she heads back to her office and keeps her head buried in work. When I ask, Ruby says Frankie is busy sorting through the inventory mess that Jessica made.

Still, she has to eat.

When three p.m. rolls around and she hasn't taken a break, I decide to bring Frankie a late lunch. I call up to the main house and ask Alain to make one of her favorite meals, but then change my mind—feeling inspired, I request a bistec sandwich and tostones for her. My hope is that the familiar comfort food will cheer her up.

But when I knock on her door and let myself into her office, she barely glances up.

"You need to eat, Frankie. I had Alain make you a special order."

"Thanks, but I already ate."

"You've been locked in here for hours," I remind her. "Take a little break."

She reaches for the sandwich and absently takes a few bites, not seeming to notice what it is. Before I can say anything more, she looks at her phone and then jumps up from her chair.

"I need to change and go lead a horseback tour. Marco's taking off early to prep for a race at the speedway. I don't want to be late."

With that, she pushes past me and strides out the door.

FRANKIE MUST BE WORKING LATE, because she doesn't show up for dinner. I immediately feel how starkly different the mood is, compared to the night prior. The table feels empty again, with just me, Armani, and Livvie present. Frankie is absent and so is Marco. Charlie, of course, is back in Nob Hill.

Livvie seems a little withdrawn, understandably. What teenage girl wants to be stuck dining with two grown men she barely knows? But since she'll be living in the guesthouse for the foreseeable future, I figure now is a good time to learn more about my youngest sister-in-law.

"Livvie, I have to say I'm impressed with the amount of training you've put into your horses," I tell her. "How did you learn so much about dressage training?"

She wipes her mouth and looks up, her eyes sparkling. I definitely started off with the right question. "YouTube."

"YouTube?"

"Yup. The trainer who I worked with for six years has a full instructional series posted." Livvie's smile wavers before she goes on, "I would've been happy to keep learning from her if not for my dad's...financial situation...but she and I still keep in touch, and her training videos are the next best thing."

"Wow," I say, genuinely taken aback. "I've seen how your Friesians go through their paces. That's an incredible accomplishment."

"Thank you," she says proudly.

I'm not being hyperbolic; the horses' movements are nearly flawless and speak to much more professional training than one would expect from a teenager using YouTube videos. Armani and I share a look.

"That's amazing, truly," Armani pipes up.

She takes a few more bites of her ravioli. "I'd like to do more with them, but I'm taking a full load of senior year classes, with a few APs that I can use for college prerequisites. Once I graduate, I'll have more time. I'd like to go to the Olympics one day."

"I didn't realize there were equestrian events at the Olympics," Armani says.

"Oh yeah," Livvie says, perking up even more. "There are over sixty-five events with horses. Dressage, Eventing, and Jumping. I don't even care if I'm not the rider, I'd just love to see some of my horses compete."

"Incredible," I say. "Have you decided where you're applying to college?" I ask. "Application deadlines are usually around, what, January or February?"

"I bet they have a great equine program at Texas A&M," Armani says. "I mean, they're known for their animal studies degrees."

Livvie stops chewing for a moment and shrugs a shoulder as she moves food around on her plate again. The shift in her attitude says I've touched a nerve.

Reading her sudden quietness as anxiety, my brother adds, "But I'm sure you can find something great here in California, if you don't want to go out of state."

"Um, it's not that," Livvie says haltingly. "College just isn't in the cards for me right now. I'm going to focus on training horses."

I voice my confusion. "Why's that? With your AP classes, your GPA has to be higher than a 4.0. And you've got plenty of equine experience. You'd get into any school you want."

She smiles warmly, but I see the defensiveness behind the warmth. "I've already qualified for a few scholarships, actually, but they barely make a dent in the tuition for the school I want. And I figure if I'm going to spend that kind of money on education, I should do it at a college I really want to attend. So I'll have to take a gap year or two. I'm hoping to get a paid job at one of the local stables or riding academies, that way I can save up my paychecks for school."

Well, that's an easy fix. I glance at Armani, who nods and then changes the subject to something more light while we finish eating.

As we all push back from the table afterward, I ask Livvie to hang on for a second.

"I have to be honest," I say. "I knew you were focused, and Frankie's always singing your praises, but I don't think I've ever met a teenager with such clear goals and self-possession."

She nods. "Thanks."

"So here's the deal," I go on. "Whatever this dream school of yours is, if you bring me your acceptance letter in the spring, the Bellanti family will cover whatever tuition your scholarships don't."

"Wha-what?"

Armani nods. "We're happy to do it. Consider it a welcome to the family gift."

I get to my feet, but almost get knocked down again by the bear hug Livvie gives me. It surprises me for a moment but then I lightly hug her back. The way these Abbott sisters are with all the hugging, I'll have to get used to it eventually.

Just then, Livvie gives out a low squeal and leaves me to race across the room. I spy Frankie in the doorway, who opens her arms as Livvie embraces her. Livvie's excited babble fills the room. Once Frankie catches on to what her sister is saying about equine programs and tuition fees, she looks over at me and Armani and mouths, "thank you." But she doesn't look thankful. She looks more upset than anything.

Livvie breaks free, saying she has homework, and gives a little wave before she leaves for the guesthouse. Armani quietly slips from the room, leaving Frankie and me by ourselves.

"I had Alain set a plate aside for you," I tell her. "It's in the kitchen. I'll get it—"

"It's fine, I can do it. I'll catch up with you later."

She forces a smile and heads into the kitchen, brushing past me without another word. I don't know how or why, but something is broken between us, and I don't know what it is.

Frustrated, I head up to my room, but I can't seem to settle my thoughts. I go to the balcony, watching the sun set as the evening, mid-October chill creeps over me. Despite the cold, I let the dark fall all around me. I'm trying—really trying—to figure out what went wrong. What I might have said or done that would've upset Frankie. I feel like there's more going on here than just Rico. And then I realize the obvious: I should just ask her. Isn't that part of the partnership she's been asking for? Open lines of communication and all of that?

The sudden glow of light from the bedroom startles me. I didn't realize how dark it had gotten. I open the French door and enter the room, hearing the bathroom door shut just as I step inside. Something about the sound of that door makes me irrationally angry.

I storm to the bathroom door, wanting nothing more than to break it down. But I take a deep breath instead and remind myself to just take it easy.

I knock, gently.

"Occupied," she says, like this is a stall in a public bathroom.

Even now, I can't hold in a huff of laughter.

"I know something's wrong, Frankie," I say through the door. "I want to fix it, but I can't even try if I don't know what it is. Will you talk to me, please?"

The door swings open. Frankie's eyes flash.

"Of course you want to fix it. You try to fix everything, even things that aren't yours to fix, like Livvie's education and my stupid marriage to Rico. But they're *my* problems to solve. I owe you too much already. You're not going to get me out of another mess."

I take her shoulders gently in my hands. "I will get you out of every mess, every time."

Her cheeks flush. "You're not even my husband. You don't owe that to me."

I don't know how to make her understand. I brush her hair away from her face, cupping her cheek in my palm. "I'm not doing it because I owe you. I'm doing it because you are everything to me, Frankie. I'll pay any price."

Something in her face changes. Her expression melts into one of relief, of realization. "I'm going to hand over my share of the Abbott Winery to you," she says. "I know it's realistically already yours because my family owes you that debt, but I want to give it to you beyond the debt. I want you to have it because I love you, and I trust you. I want you to have it because I want...because I want you to have all of me."

"What a gift you are to me," I say.

I crush her to me, my heart so full I can barely breathe.

25

FRANKIE

Is this really happening?

Have I finally found a man that I can rely on? One who actually solves problems instead of causing them?

After the whole Rico situation blew up in my face, I never even dreamed of finding a man who didn't cause more trouble than he was worth, but I'm starting to believe that such a thing is possible. As Dante holds me, I realize that I can trust Dante not just with my life, but with Livvie's as well, and Charlie's if it comes down to it. He's going to take care of us.

Not out of obligation or for personal gain, but because he wants to.

Because he loves me.

"I love you, Dante," I whisper, my head pressed against his chest so tightly that I can hear his heartbeat. "I love you so much."

He leans down to kiss my forehead, my eyelids, my

jaw, my throat, every soft press of his lips drawing tingles over my skin.

"I love you," he says into my neck. Then he pulls back to look into my eyes. "I *need* you. In my life. In my bed. In my heart. I love you, Francesca Bellanti."

My eyes are tearing up, but I manage a bittersweet little laugh. "I don't have your name anymore, remember?"

He begins unbuttoning my blouse. "You have all of me. All of me. Always."

I'm tempted to help him undress me, but I hold still and let him do the work. I love the brush of his fingers against my skin and how intently he focuses on each button, clasp, and zipper. His movements are careful today—no ripping fabric or popping buttons. Closing my eyes, I absorb the sound and feel and scent of him as he strips me bare.

"Now you can watch me," he whispers as he trails a finger along my jaw.

Happy to obey, I take in the glorious sight of him reaching across his body and pulling his T-shirt over his head. My gaze devours his sculpted torso, the mouthwatering ripples of his tight abs, the light trail of hair leading down the waistband of his pants. A hot ache twists at my core as he works the waistband over his narrow hips, down his muscled thighs, and then finally steps out of them.

His perfect, rigid cock is like a work of art, something I'll never get tired of seeing.

"You like that?" he asks, a smirk on his face.

"Why don't you put your clothes back on and do it all over again," I tease.

Laughing, he spreads me out on the bed, then gazes down at me appreciatively. I raise myself up on my elbows so I can do the same to him.

"What else do you like, Francesca? What do you want me to do to you?"

I don't get the chance to answer before he begins kissing his way up my body, oh so slowly. Kiss by kiss, caress by caress, ankle to knee to the curve of my hip. A thorough study.

He runs his tongue around each areola while his palms skim over my ribs, down my belly, and back up to cup my breasts. Then he moves his mouth over my nipples one at a time, licking and sucking, tugging softly with his teeth. I can barely breathe I'm panting so hard, grabbing the sheets as I squirm with need. His touch is the biggest aphrodisiac.

By the time his lips finally reach my own, I'm a puddle of need. I arch my hips, pushing up against his erection with desperate thrusts, but he holds himself back on purpose.

"Give it to me," I beg.

"Tell me what you want," he commands.

"I just did."

"Say it."

"I want you," I pant. "Inside me."

Our lips meet and I forget the whole conversation, until he pulls away and nuzzles his nose against my neck, the tip of his dick still brushing my entrance. It's maddening.

"Be more specific," he says.

God, what this man does to me. "I want to get railed by your fucking cock."

Grasping for him, I huff my frustration when he moves his hips out of reach.

"Tell me."

"Dammit, what do you want from me?" I ask, only half kidding. "I want to fuck! Screw. Bang. *Peen* in *vageen.* Is that clear enough for you?"

Dante starts cackling with laughter, and I can't help joining in. He kisses me again, at first in between our chuckles and then deeper, slower, as if he wants to be a part of me. I could almost come just from the feel of his tongue on mine.

I spread my legs wider in invitation and Dante finally grants my request, sliding into me in the hottest, most unhurried, deliberate stroke I have ever felt. He moves slowly, too slowly, torturing me on purpose. When he's fully sheathed, I wrap my legs around his waist and purr like a cat.

"That's perfect," I tell him. My body is tight with frustration, eager for more. But instead of picking up his pace, he stops what he's doing, staying exactly where he is.

"What else do you want me to do?" he prods.

"I want more." He doesn't move. I think I hate this game. "Thrust faster, damn you."

He does. I arch up to meet him as pleasure explodes through me.

"What else?"

"Harder," I pant.

Dante pushes my knees up to my chest so he can get a better angle, and he starts ramming into me even deeper, harder, faster, giving new meaning to the term jackhammering. But I love it. I want it. He's giving me exactly what I asked for...and then he stops.

"What? No, no, no. I didn't say stop!"

He's breathing hard as he grabs my chin. "Tell me. What do you need?"

I pout. "Cross your damn eyes."

His eyebrows lift, and then he crosses his eyes and sticks out the tip of his tongue for good measure.

"Oh my God, you!" I gasp, laughing. He laughs too, and I swear I can feel his joy wrapping around me like a security blanket. I love this thing between us.

Even so, a girl has needs. And it's getting worse by the second.

Taking his face between my hands, I give him a serious-not-serious look. "Please, please, please. I beg you. Get the fucking job done, Bellanti."

The amusement on his face is replaced by pure lust as he uses those talented hip swings to work us both toward oblivion. We're moaning each other's names, making a mess of the bed, heedless of the headboard knocking fast and loud against the wall. All I can do is cling to him tight and voice my approval as we both slide into wave after wave of pleasure—and okay, fuck, he does get the job done. When we come, we come hard.

Afterward, we lay there together, cooling in the afterglow.

WHEN I WAKE in the predawn darkness, I'm momentarily disoriented. My brain says it's morning, but the sky doesn't. It takes me a second to remember it's late fall now, and that the sun has been rising later and later each day.

Breathing deeply, trying to slow my rapid heartbeat, I snuggle back against Dante's warm body. His hands rove over my stomach, smoothing down the curve of my hip, and they anchor me in the darkness.

I feel safe. Protected. By this man.

Who knew he could be so loving? So silly. So joyful.

I still resent my father for selling me off—I'll never be grateful for *that*—but I am grateful that even if I didn't choose Dante, he might just turn out to be a very good man. I feel the glow of love filling my cheeks, my chest, my belly. By some miracle, something between us has radically changed. Something almost too good to be true has happened. But I'm too tired and too content to wonder how it came to be. Happy is happy.

And I am so damn happy with Dante.

My eyes have just fluttered shut again when I feel his hand slip between my thighs, his finger tracing little circles around my opening until I'm wet and buzzing. With a soft moan, I shift my body so he can dip his finger inside, but instead he glides into me from behind, his cock sliding in easily like a key in a lock.

"Mmm," I moan.

He moves his hand, spreading it across my lower belly, holding me steady as he pushes deeper inside, rooting himself deep. I gasp, then sigh at how perfectly he fills me. Dante begins to move, taking his pleasure, and I grind my ass back in time with his thrusts, meeting each one with a hissing intake of breath.

He's fucking me steady and deep, his movements gradually becoming faster, harder, and more insistent. His hand slides up to cup my breast, and he works my nipples until I'm panting.

"These are mine. Mine," he groans.

"Yes," I whimper as he shifts his angle to hit the spot that always sets me off.

Possessive words of love and adoration continue pouring from his lips. "This is my ass, my sweet little cunt."

"Yes, Dante."

"Mine," he says.

"Yours."

Reaching behind me, my hands find their way to the back of his head, pulling him even closer against me.

"Mine." He thrusts. "Mine." Again. "All mine." Again, again, again...

"*Yes*. Yours. All yours." I agree with every word, and

then I'm coming apart in an unstoppable tumble, the orgasm flooding over me, so hard and deep it brings tears to my eyes. I weave my fingers into his hair and hang on as I soak in the pleasure. *"Yours, yours, yours."*

I never want to be anything else.

26

FRANKIE

"No MATTER WHAT happens in there, promise that you'll trust me," Dante says.

We're heading down to the Bellanti offices the next morning, and my arm is linked with his. That arm might be the only solid thing anchoring me right now.

The Bellanti lawyers have finished reviewing the divorce paperwork and contract that Rico presented to us, and we're meeting up with him to settle this once and for all. I'm cautiously optimistic, but I'm also a bundle of nerves. I also can't shake the nagging feeling that there's something Dante isn't sharing with me, but I don't press. I do trust him, and I tell him so.

He kisses the top of my head. "Good. We're going to get through this. I promise."

And just like that, I believe him. We *are* going to get through this. Together.

I take a deep breath and admire the view of the vineyard as we step outside and onto the gravel path that leads to the offices. The day is young, but the air is crisp and the sun is bright and it's clearly going to be a gorgeous one. Maybe it's an omen. Suddenly, I feel confident.

Which lasts about as long as it takes to enter the Bellanti offices, where we're met by a smiling Rico. Does he have an ace up his sleeve, or is he just happy to be getting the payoff he's been dreaming of? I'm sure it's thrilling for him to know he's about to become a millionaire.

The smile evaporates from my face, and the day seems a lot less bright.

Raising the steaming mug that's in his hand, Rico says, "Ruby made me coffee. She said we are meeting in the conference room. Now?"

Other than Ruby, the offices are empty of employees. It's early, just a few minutes after eight o'clock. Dante thought it would be best to get this meeting over with before the rest of the staff arrived so they wouldn't ask questions.

He inclines his head and gestures for Rico to follow us down the long hallway. I grind my teeth and try to pretend the scumbag isn't inches away from me. I'd like nothing more than to punch that stupid grin right off his face.

Once we get to the conference room, Rico takes the seat at the head of the table and slouches in the chair with the smug posture of a man who owns the place. No doubt, he believes he's about to come into a windfall. How presumptuous. Especially considering the fact that

Marco is sitting in the chair beside him, wearing a bespoke suit and a menacing expression. I know he's probably here purely for show, and maybe to keep Rico in line, but I'm glad to have his support.

Dante pulls out a chair for me on the other end of the table and sits next to me. We clasp hands and I make myself take a slow, deep breath.

"So. Should we begin?" Rico says eagerly, smoothing his tie.

Typical Rico, trying to take control of the situation. But no matter. It's obvious that Dante's the one in charge —since everyone in the room is looking at him, waiting for him to get the ball rolling.

Just then, Armani appears in the doorway and leans against it. I see him shake his head at Dante, who responds with a slight nod. I have no idea what it means, but it comforts me. Marco's gaze gets even more hard and focused, a slight smile on his face, and Rico looks between the three brothers and suddenly sits upright.

"Let's get started," Dante says, his voice steely.

Clearing his throat nervously, Rico pulls his copy of the divorce papers out of his jacket and slides them across the table toward me and Dante, just out of reach.

"If you can just give me my check, I will sign off on the divorce and be on my way. That is best for everyone, you see?" Rico babbles. "I have always dreamed of buying a villa on the island of Sardinia. Getting a boat, too, and fishing every day. Swordfish and snapper. Maybe I will open a restaurant on the beach! How lucky I am, to have married into such a rich family."

His gloating is unbearable. But as he blathers on about all his plans for the money, I start to realize that the reason he must have left me in the first place wasn't because he couldn't take care of me—it was because *I* couldn't take care of him.

It all makes sense now. After we got married, he started pressing me about us buying a house together, and asking how much money I thought my father would send as a "wedding gift" for our new home. When I finally confessed that my family was broke, Rico had acted like it made no difference to him. But sure enough...he'd skipped out on me, just days later.

Jesus. He'd only married me because he thought he was marrying into wealth. Generational wealth. American vineyard family wealth. And when things didn't pan out, he left me alone in a foreign country.

Until he suddenly shows up *again*, exploiting me *again*, coincidentally popping up in my hometown the moment my fortunes have reversed. Likely thanks to stalking me on social media.

Rico's done talking, apparently. I haven't been paying attention, but he's staring at me as if expecting some kind of response. He glances at Dante. "Do you need to go get your checkbook, or...?"

Dante gives my hand a squeeze and slowly stands up. He reaches for the divorce papers on the table, picks them up, and then—right in front of Rico's eyes—rips the papers down the middle. Then he places them back on the table.

I'm not sure who's more shocked—me, or Rico.

Has Dante been lying to me? Does he not want me at all? Maybe he's changed his mind. Maybe I'm not worth the price...

"What was that for? I am going to have to get new copies made!" Rico looks like he's about to stand from his seat, but Armani stops him with a firm hand on his arm.

Dante coolly says, "Your marriage to Frankie wasn't recorded in any *Ufficio dello Stato Civile* anywhere in Italy. Nor were any marriage certificates filed with any government, US or Italian. You two were never, ever married. Not legally, anyway."

"*What?*" I whisper, my heart stuttering in my chest.

"That's a lie," Rico says. "I have the documents—"

"You have jack shit," Marco cuts in, grinning.

"And you are legally entitled to precisely nothing," Armani adds.

Rico's eyes dart from Bellanti to Bellanti. "This is a bluff. The marriage is legal. I can get you the papers," he insists, his voice pitching higher with panic.

Dante doesn't even blink. "You're welcome to try, but falsifying marriage documents is a crime. In your country and mine. My legal team would, of course, be happy to prosecute you to the full extent of the law."

I rack my brain, recalling our quick, cheap ceremony. The "priest" that Rico hired from the village...an elderly man who barely spoke outside of asking us to recite our vows...I never questioned whether he was ordained or not.

Rico had staged the entire thing from the very beginning.

The dilapidated country church that he thought would be so quaint. The paperwork I signed after the ceremony—it was in Italian, and I skimmed it, but I hadn't actually given it a thorough read. I just assumed it had been a legal standard marriage certificate.

How the hell could I have been so stupid?

"You're lying!" Rico fumes. "What kind of game is this?"

Dante shrugs. "You tell us."

"I married her in a church," Rico insists, getting belligerent. "With a priest present! It was legal!"

Marco stands and crosses his arms over his chest, looking like he's ready to crack some skulls. Rico glances up, and seeing Marco looming over him seems to set him off even more.

"Listen to me," Rico says. "I did not want it to come to this, but you leave me no choice. I have photos of Francesca...*compromising* photos, that it would be a shame for anyone to see if I were to post them on the—"

Before he can even finish, Marco is dragging him out of his seat and planting a fist in his jaw, knocking Rico to the floor. He tries to scramble to his feet, but Marco and Armani grab him first, lifting him up and slamming him back down in the chair. He tries to wriggle out of their grasp, but their iron grips stay locked on his shoulders.

It's all too much. My face is hot. I feel like I might pass out.

Dante kneels beside me and takes my hand. "Frankie, did you know about the photographs?" His voice is soft, tender. Like I've been injured and he's tending to me.

I shake my head. "No. If he took any, it wasn't with my permission."

With a nod, Dante stands again. "What you're threatening to do is another crime, Correa. I think you're lying about those photos, but if you aren't, and they should somehow find their way onto the Internet, there is no country you can hide in where I will not find you—and *end you*. It's time for you to leave California. Never come back."

Rico isn't given a chance to argue. Marco and Armani just pick him up like a rag doll and drag him out the door. His sputtering and cursing echo down the hall until suddenly, it's quiet.

Dante sits down next to me again, reaches into his jacket, and pulls out a new document.

"What is that?" I murmur as he sets it on the conference table in front of me.

"It's a marriage settlement. Read it. It ensures that if Correa, or your father, or anyone else *ever* tries to come after the Abbott Winery or any of its assets, the law has them wrapped up firmly with the Bellanti family holdings."

Dante waits patiently while I pore over the contract, my finger following along with every sentence, my heart flooding in my chest as I slowly parse the legal verbiage.

Another marriage for us. A fresh start. A chance at a real union this time.

No matter my sisters' or my marital status, no one can take over the winery. And speaking of my sisters, he's worked in a profit-sharing clause regarding the Abbott portion of the wine sales. Which means that even though Charlie still has her job, her income won't have to rely solely on getting contracted for large events; she'll have steady money coming in from her cut of the profits. So will Livvie—and she won't have to give up on her horses or her Olympic dreams, either. Because the land transfer includes the Abbott stables.

I have to wait until the tears swimming in my eyes clear to find the signature line on the last page. Looking at Dante, I ask, "Are you sure about this?"

He smiles. "I meant it when I said any price." He takes a pen from his breast pocket and holds it out to me. "Be mine, Frankie. For real this time."

I take the pen and glance away from him just long enough to sign my name on the dotted line before throwing myself in his arms.

I'm so glad that my husband—my *real* husband—always comes through.

27

FRANKIE

WHEN CHARLIE HAD ORIGINALLY PITCHED the masquerade theme for the End of Harvest Gala, I wasn't quite sure what to expect. But I trust her creative process, and boy, has it paid off.

She's gone all out, turning Bellanti Vineyards into a spooky themed wonderland. The trees are decorated in blinking white, gold, and purple fairy lights. Glittery cobwebs ethereally drape the branches. There are also glowing crystal balls lining the walkways, flickering like magic as you pass by. Hidden speakers play a variety of classic haunted house sounds that you can hear whenever the band takes a break. It's literally breathtaking.

Our guests have gone all out with their costumes, too. I see fantastical ball gowns in gleaming jewel tones, silk and velvet suits, top hats and veils and Victorian-style fascinators, and white porcelain masks all around. Charlie created brick walkways throughout the property and installed temporary lampposts decorated with potted geraniums, which give the party an old-world feel. The chilly evening breeze blows softly, scattering around the scent of the many flowers decorating the scene.

There are black and purple roses in large urns, and a Queen of Hearts garden similar to the one in *Alice in Wonderland.* It's basically genius—black and white harlequin floor tiles lead to a row of white rose bushes and a table of small buckets of red paint with little brushes for guests to paint the roses.

We're hoping the event will be successful enough to kick off another fabulous new tradition, whereby Bellanti Vineyards will be known for hosting an annual masquerade ball. And considering that the tickets were a few hundred dollars each, we really need to pull this off without a hitch. But I don't think we'll have any problems. It's obvious that everyone's having a fabulous time.

I make my way through the crowd, daintily holding the stick of my mask as I keep it pressed against my eyes. I'm wearing a lavish plum and burgundy taffeta gown with a plunging neckline and a low back. Frilly fronds of lace hang off the three-quarter-sleeves, while the hoops make my skirts bob and sway as I walk.

Browsing the crowd for Dante, I take my time greeting the guests and stopping to make small talk. He'd barely left my side all evening but then got pulled away by some associates he wanted to schmooze. I finally see the top of his dark head over the crowd and begin heading that way when there's a sudden, delighted shout from behind me.

Just then, a thudding sound vibrates the ground.

Everyone turns to scan the darkness of the vineyard as a huge black horse races toward the crowd. Its ghostly, apparently headless rider is dressed in white and holds a flaming torch high in the air. A grin splits my face.

Livvie canters a stalwart Ytoo just close enough to the crowd to give them a delightful fright. She lets out a trilling yell as she passes by and then disappears into the shadows with the train of her white gown trailing behind her. There's a collective breath, and then everyone claps.

A few seconds later, she appears on the other side, and then races again into the darkness. There's another cheer, and the servers begin rotating trays of a select vintage through the crowd as the guests watch eagerly for the headless phantom to reappear. But Livvie keeps them in anticipation as she gallops close enough to be heard but not seen, the eerie sound of her ghostly cry fading into the night air.

"Everyone's going to be talking about that for months." Dante comes up behind me and gives a salute with his wine glass in Livvie's direction. "Should I be worried at how well she pulls off being a specter?"

I grab his glass and take a sip. "She can pull off anything as long as she's on the back of a horse."

"She's talented, like her sister." Dante kisses me on the temple.

"You mean, *sisters*. Charlie did a hell of a job."

"Agreed. She's about to become very popular, and very busy. I've already had several inquiries into who planned the Gala."

Looping my hands around his neck, I push up on my

tiptoes for a kiss. "You can't imagine how happy that makes me. I'd love for Charlie to be overrun with clients."

His arms wrap around me. He looks amazing in his custom suit with long tails, and a crisp, high-collared shirt with small pearl buttons. He tucked his mask into his pocket earlier and I'm glad, because it means I have an unobstructed view of his perfect face.

"You know what I want?" he asks in a husky whisper that sends liquid heat straight between my legs.

"No, but I have a pretty good guess."

"I bet you do. And as soon as the midnight toast is over, I intend to show you exactly what I have in mind."

"Promises, promises." I tap the tip of his nose with my finger. "Promises I expect you to keep, sir."

"Anything for you, madam," he says, giving me a sweeping, low bow.

After kissing the back of my hand, he straightens to his full height. Adjusting his top hat, he blows me a kiss and disappears into the crowd. A moment later, he appears on the stage beneath a canopy of crisscrossed strings of twinkling fairy lights with a microphone in his hand.

He addresses the crowd and asks them to please grab a champagne flute as the servers move through the group. While that's being accomplished, he calls Charlie's name.

"I'd like to introduce the incredibly talented event planner who is responsible for every aspect of tonight's Gala. Well, everything but the wine, of course."

I smile at the tone of his voice, teasingly light, as if he's finally getting the hang of telling jokes. Charlie makes her way through the crowd as they clap and cheer for her. She takes her place beside Dante on the stage and he sings her praises. My heart swells with gratitude and love for them both.

Once all the champagne has been passed around, Dante makes a toast to our guests, the winery, and the success of the harvest season. Everyone drinks to that and the band resumes playing. Cradling my glass in my hand, I sit at the edge of the crowd and take it all in. This night has been truly magical. I can't think of one thing that would have made it better.

Looking up, I spy Dante walking toward me, his expression intense and striking. My breath hitches, my nipples perking instantly at the lust on his face. Oh, yes. His promise.

His delicious promise.

Reaching for my hand, he lifts me to my feet. "Follow me, please."

I twine my fingers with his and do a double take when I realize he's leading me away from the party. "Should we be leaving now?"

"The party will be raging on until the wee hours, I'm sure, but Charlie and the rest of the staff have everything well in hand. No one will notice that we've slipped away. Besides, if they knew what I had in mind, they wouldn't blame us."

My heart flutters as he leads me to the main house, up the stairs, and out on the balcony off of his room. We can't see the band or any of the festivities up here, but the music floats up toward us, as if from an invisible band, punctuated by the faint sounds of laughter. Dante spins me across the balcony, then gathers me against him tight and begins a slow dance in time to the music. His body feels so good, so comforting as he easily moves me around the small space.

"I've been waiting for this moment all night," he whispers huskily against my ear.

He tenderly caresses the bare skin on my back where the dress dips low. Resting my cheek against his solid chest, I breathe peacefully with the thought that this is my life now. This man, once so cold and rigid, has learned how to open up to me. We've struggled and clashed, separated and reunited, but somehow we ended up exactly where we were supposed to be.

Our dancing becomes closer, tighter, his teeth gently worrying my earlobe. I suck in a breath, letting my head fall back as I drink in the sensation. His lips move to cruise my cheek, my jaw, my neck. Chills race over me.

"Do you trust me?" he whispers.

A soft moan works from my throat. "With my life."

He slowly backs me up until the balcony's balustrade presses into my lower back. Gripping my hips, he lifts me and sets me onto the wide railing. I know I'm secure, but with nothing to break my fall, the yawning blackness behind me drives my pulse to the moon. Yet even as my heart jacks, I'm not afraid. Dante won't let anything happen to me.

With one arm locked securely around me, Dante slips his hand underneath the fluff of my taffeta skirt, up my leg, and then urges my thighs apart. My knees go weak, and I grip the rail tighter for support. When he slides his finger straight into me, I jerk in response, my body going into overdrive with that one simple touch.

"You're always so hot for me, Francesca," he murmurs, slipping another finger inside. "So hot...so wet..."

He starts working my clit with his thumb, making small circles just the way I like. It's impossible for me to stay completely still, yet I'm acutely aware of the thirty-foot drop below. Tossing my head back, I grip the rail harder even as Dante tightens his grip on me.

"I've got you," he says, fingering me faster. "Just let go."

And I do.

Because even though I'm high above the ground, I know I'm in no danger of falling. Dante will always catch me. Be my solid ground, my foundation.

A hard shiver goes through me as the twisting heat between my legs reaches a peak. I grab his shoulders tight and look into his eyes, moaning his name softly so he knows how close I am, and suddenly I can't hold back. Coming hard and deep, I fall into the orgasm like I'm free-falling, riding his fingers like they're his dick. My whole world is nothing but white-hot pleasure.

As I float back down to earth, I realize I'm still in his arms, his cock sliding ever so slowly inside me until I'm completely full of him. He lets out a long breath and then starts thrusting, faster and faster. Clinging to him, I muffle my moans in the fabric of his jacket as he pounds into me, pushing me to the precipice of another release.

With a groan, Dante picks me up, still inside me, and spins us around so he can push my back against the wall of the house. I wrap my legs around him, tilting my hips, drawing him deeper. So deep, I can't keep quiet anymore. As soft whimpers spill from my lips, Dante pushes into me harder and harder, fucking me so good I can barely stand it, the pleasure ratcheting up, up, tighter, harder. Higher. It's like we're dancing again, our bodies in perfect sync.

Suddenly, I'm tipping into oblivion once more, my cries pitching higher and more desperate as I gush around Dante's cock. With a fierce moan, Dante comes inside me, holding me tightly to him as he shudders his release. And then we're kissing again, whispering words of love, bathed in silvery moonlight as the distant music wraps itself around us.

It's perfect. He's perfect.

Everything about this night is perfection.

FRANKIE

I just love giving money away.

It took the whole weekend to recover from the Gala, but now it's Monday and I'm well rested and ready to dive back into work.

The staff is gathered in the tasting room for a briefing, and I've just addressed them with congratulations for putting on such an extremely successful event—followed by my gleeful announcement about the bonuses they'll each be receiving out of the vineyard's profits. The looks of shock and delight on their faces fills me with joy. They've earned it, and I'm glad Dante agreed to giving them something in return for their hard work.

He's standing in the back, observing and clearly letting me take the spotlight on this. I'm glad to do it. This is *my* staff, after all.

"I have one more announcement," I call above the excited hum. Locking eyes with Greg, I motion him over. "I've enjoyed my time working here with all of you, but moving forward, I'll be spending the bulk of my time on back-of-house details. So, I'm promoting Greg from tasting room manager to tasting room director—he'll basically be getting a well-deserved raise, and hiring someone else as his assistant manager. So get those resumes polished up, team."

Another cheer goes up. Greg's cheeks grow pink as he gives a little bow.

"But that's not all," I say. "Greg, you want to tell them your news?"

I step back, and he moves to the front of the room.

"Thank you so much. And everyone, I do apologize for missing the Gala—but I had a pretty good reason." He glances at me with a smile. "I'm happy to say that I've completed my Sommelier qualifications."

The staff starts applauding and shouting their congratulations, and the meeting breaks up as everyone rushes to surround Greg with love and support. I give his arm a squeeze and slip off to the side, watching everyone until Dante appears beside me.

Kissing the top of my head, he slips an arm around my waist and says, "I have to run into town for a meeting at the bank. But I'll meet you at home for dinner...and dessert."

He gives my ass a covert squeeze before stepping away.

I can already feel my cheeks heating as my mind fills with all the things I want to do to him—and have done to me. I wonder if I could sneak a can of whipped cream from the refrigerator later...

Realizing how late it's getting, I say my goodbyes and try to banish my dirty thoughts as I head to my office. The halls are quiet today, as if everyone is still basking in the success of the Gala. Pausing outside my door, I smile at the new name plate on the wall. *Francesca Bellanti.*

I run a finger over the engraved lettering. Finally, a name I can be proud of.

Settling in at my desk, I start going over the merger paperwork for Bellanti Vineyards and the Abbott Winery again. There's a bunch of legalese that I can't fully parse —the finer points of merging one business to another. In the back are unofficial-looking typed notes, probably the work of Jessica when she was still assisting Dante. I also come across some cursory agreements for what look like personal loans and their repayment terms, but I quickly flip past those pages since they don't seem applicable to the merger. Until a name jumps out at me.

Abbott Winery.

My stomach churns.

I'm holding in my hands the original deal that my father made with Dante—the agreement whereby my father turned over our family winery *and me* as payment of his debts.

Disgusted, I let the stack of papers fall on top of the ugly, offending page. I don't want to read this document. Don't want to know how much money my father sold me for.

But even as I tell myself that, a perverse curiosity is taking over, my fingers flipping through the stack as I look for the page.

Exactly how much did my piece of shit father think I was actually worth?

The page appears and my eyes track the document for currency. There, almost at the end. I read the number, then read it again. I can't believe it. There must be a mistake. Missing zeroes. Something.

$286,000 stares at me in black and white.

I swallow, but my throat is dry.

$286,000.

There's ringing in my ears, and I feel like the ground is dropping out from under me.

The Abbott Winery is easily worth twenty times that...and yet my father had traded it *along with his fucking daughter* for $286,000.

That fucking dumbass shit-for-brains. Fucking unbelievable. Fucking...

I slam the whole file folder closed, cram it back into my filing cabinet, and shove the drawer back into the cabinet with a bang.

Two hundred eighty six thousand...fuck.

The number can't help but stick in my mind, the thought of it making me sick to my stomach. I wish I'd never looked.

Trying to shake it off, I return to the binders full of Bellanti Vineyards' financials that I started looking through last week. I pore over the paperwork, hoping to distract myself with all the numbers, working backwards from the end of the last quarter—when Enzo had died.

God, have I really only been married to Dante for a few months? It feels like entire lifetimes have passed.

Like I've died and risen from the ashes more times than I can count.

I flip to a fresh page and find a single sheet that seems to be a list of debt forgiveness statements and loans to be forgiven, to be released upon the death of Enzo Bellanti. The typed lines are in some kind of code, strings of letters and numbers attached to dollar amounts, but one number —a total listed as $286,000—screams at me from the page.

There are no actual names listed on the statements, just the codes.

I press the intercom button. "Ruby, can I borrow you for a moment, please?"

A minute later she comes in, holding a steaming cup of coffee. "Good morning, Mrs. Bellanti. I thought you might like a fresh coffee."

"Thank you, Ruby."

She sets it on the desk with a smile that quickly fades when I hold up the sheet.

"Can you tell me what these codes mean?" I ask.

Suddenly flustered, she works her fingers before reaching for the page. "Oh, that's...that's nothing, Mrs. Bellanti. Let me take that."

Her face pales as I pull the page out of her reach, holding her off.

"I need to know, Ruby," I say, keeping my voice as calm as possible, but my tone brooking no arguments. "What. Is. This."

We lock eyes for a moment, but she looks away

nervously. A tense smile plays on her lips, but it doesn't last. Finally, she sinks into the chair opposite me.

"Yes, well, I—I suppose you are a Bellanti now," she says haltingly. "So that page is...it's from the old business. The way the family originally made their money. Personal loans, some betting books, not all of it...you know. On the up and up. So to speak."

"Shady stuff," I supply.

Some of the color returns to her face and she nods. "When Mr. Bellanti Senior passed, his sons wanted to be rid of his more...sordid affairs. So they forgave some debts to get them off the record, and then started negotiating with the Bruno family to sell off the gambling books."

I lean across the desk and hold the page out, pointing to the line concerning my family's debt. "And this deal?"

She glances at the number quickly and then clears her throat. "That deal was, um, kept out for some reason."

"Ruby," I ask, my voice devoid of emotion, "is this my father's debt?"

Her eyes drop to the floor. "Yes, ma'am. It looks like it."

A hollow feeling starts to gnaw inside me. "And the Bellantis were going to forgive it?"

"The Brunos wouldn't have been interested in that one. They only wanted the debts related to the horse races or the auto tracks, so they told the Bellantis to keep the rest, cash in on whatever else was left. It was only around a million or so in personal loans. But Dante didn't want to chase the money down, so he had them all forgiven instead. Or I guess, all but this one. I'm afraid I don't know more than that."

The emptiness yawns wide inside me as the solid world that I'd been so sure of drops away, leaving me flailing once more.

"Thank you, Ruby. You can go."

She leaves without a word. I pull the mug of coffee on my desk closer, trying to warm my hands on the ceramic. My entire body feels like ice.

Dante...he organized all of it. If he didn't want to forgive my father's debt, he could have at least settled it.

In fact, if he had waited just a few more months, I would have been home from Italy already and firmly in control of the Abbott Winery's finances and business operations. Dante could have approached me with a proposal—a financial one—and I could have brokered a deal to square my family's debt that would have the Bellantis paid off in a year or two.

The Abbott women would have still owned our family winery.

If only my father had...

But now...

...oh, God.

I've signed it all away to Dante.

And that profit sharing he offered to me and my sisters—profit sharing that I'd been oh so grateful for—pales in comparison to the money we could have potentially been making if I'd been allowed to keep the winery and turn it around. But I didn't know I was being played.

Dante played me.

A wave of dizziness washes over me, my hands get clammy, sudden nausea burning in my throat. I'm going to be sick.

I bolt from the office, barely making it to the restroom before I vomit up my breakfast. My middle heaves again and again until I'm spent. Washing out my mouth at the sink afterward, I realize that the golden palace I thought I lived in is really a gilded cage.

$286,000.

My father sold me, our family's livelihood, and his daughters' futures away for just over a quarter of a million dollars.

And Dante...God, what a fucking fool I've been. How expertly he's manipulated me, every step of the way, from day one.

He made me believe he loved me, all so he could maneuver me into signing away my family's fortune. Sure, he's still attentive now, but how long will that even last? Clearly he gets off on having power over me. Controlling me.

I think back on how well he had faked being in love with me at the pressing event, even though he was furious at me. He was so very good at fooling people. A fucking expert at it.

Another memory comes to me: the image of Jessica through the window of the main house, on her knees, sucking cock. Dante, encouraging her in Italian.

He's been lying to me the whole time.

Letting out a deep breath, I blot my face with a paper towel and look in the mirror.

Goddamn, I am so tired of the men in my life. And what a fucking fool love has turned me into. So eager for affection that I'd wrecked my life—twice now.

I can't do this anymore. I need to get away. Far away. Somewhere Dante will never find me. Because I'll never clear my head if I'm anywhere near him, or the Bellanti property.

On my way back up to the main house, I text Charlie and ask her to pick up Livvie at school and bring her back to the Nob Hill house. I promise to explain later.

In Dante's room, once more, I pack a bag—quickly realizing there isn't much to take, because I hardly own anything that Dante's money hasn't bought me. I take the bare minimum, along with my makeup and toiletries, and then I borrow a few hundred in cash from the home budget safe with a note that says it was me who took it.

Gripping the keys to the Jaguar for dear life, I toss my bag into the back seat and get in. I don't look at the house or give what I'm about to do a second thought.

As I peel out of there, I leave the biggest dust cloud I possibly can on my way out of this hell.

Dante and Frankie's story concludes in Broken Trust...

You can't run from the past... or from a Bellanti.

I've always been a foolish girl.
I should have learned my lesson the first time a man betrayed me.

It hurt when Rico abandoned me. My father's deal was agony.

Dante's betrayal... it might kill me.

And there's nothing I can do.
He's not the kind of man who takes orders from his wife.
And he'll never let me leave.
There's nowhere I can go that he won't find me.

My father forced me to marry him.

Dante made me love him.

It's my turn to show them all what a Bellanti woman is...

Find out what happens in Broken Trust.

The Bellanti Brothers

Dante

Broken Bride

Broken Vow

Broken Trust

ABOUT THE AUTHOR

Stella Gray is an emerging author of contemporary romance. When she is not writing, Stella loves to read, hike, knit and cuddle with her greyhound.

Made in United States
North Haven, CT
31 October 2021

10721659R00152